W9-CLB-877

Showdown at the Alamo!

"On the count of three," said Sweetboy. "Go for a speed-loader."

"One."

Harry felt sweat appear on his forehead. The San Antonio night was hot. The interior of the Alamo was hotter. His Magnum seemed to get heavier and heavier.

"Two."

His leg began to throb. He suddenly couldn't remember whether his jacket pocket had flaps or not.

"Three!"

Harry's right thumb was kicking the Magnum's cylinder open as his left arm dug into his jacket pocket....

Books by Dane Hartman

Dirty Harry #1: Duel For Cannons
Dirty Harry #2: Death on the Docks

Published by
WARNER BOOKS

CALLING ALL MEN OF ACTION...

Please drop us a card with your name and address and we'll keep
you up-to-date on all the great forthcoming books in our MEN OF
ACTION series – you'll know in advance what is coming out so you
won't miss any of these exciting adventures We would also enjoy
your comments on the books you have read. Send to: SPECIAL
SALES DEPARTMENT, WARNER BOOKS, 75 ROCKEFELLER
PLAZA, NEW YORK, N Y 10019

ARE THERE WARNER BOOKS
YOU WANT BUT CANNOT FIND IN YOUR LOCAL STORES?

You can get any WARNER BOOKS title in print. Simply send title
and retail price, plus 50¢ per order and 20¢ per copy to cover
mailing and handling costs for each book desired New York State
and California residents add applicable sales tax Enclose check
or money order only, no cash please, to: WARNER BOOKS, P O
BOX 690, NEW YORK, N.Y 10019

DIRTY HARRY #1

Duel for Cannons

Dane Hartman

WARNER BOOKS

A Warner Communications Company

WARNER BOOKS EDITION

Copyright © 1981 by Warner Books, Inc.
All rights reserved.

Warner Books, Inc., 75 Rockefeller Plaza, New York, N.Y. 10019

 A Warner Communications Company

Printed in the United States of America

First Printing: September, 1981

10 9 8 7 6 5 4 3 2 1

Dedication

To Harry's very spirit:
Clint Eastwood and Don Siegel

Acknowledgments

Jim Trupin
Ed Breslin
Art Bourgeau
Steve Hartov
Harry Julian Fink
Dean Riesner
Michael Cimino
John Milius
The San Antonio *Star*
The Fairfield Connecticut Police Department
Melissa

DIRTY HARRY #1

Duel for Cannons

One

Boopsie's head exploded. One second the cartoon character was bending down to shake the little girl's hand, the next second hunks of thick, painted plastic were flying off in all directions.

Sheriff Boris Tucker didn't see the bullet smash into the character's head. The person in the Boopsie suit had just leaned in front of him to talk to his daughter when it happened. All Tucker knew was that his little girl was screaming in pain and that their vacation was over. It was only after Boopsie fell over and Tucker had pulled his Bulldog .44 Special from his waistband that the sheriff noted the gaping holes in both sides of the character's head.

Tucker noticed a lot of things as he automatically scanned the area. He noticed that one of the holes in the Boopsie head was fairly round and small as compared to the big, jagged hole in the other side. He noticed that a thin stream of blood had begun to drool out of the jagged side. He noticed that several plastic pieces had spun out into his daughter's face, leaving several cuts. He noticed

9

that his stunned wife had gathered their daughter into her arms and was desperately trying to soothe the howling girl. And he noticed a big, dark-haired man in dirty white overalls shouldering his way through the gathering crowd of onlookers. He noticed the man's right arm moving as if pushing something into his overall pocket.

The last thing he noted before going after that man was his wife's pale face. Her expression was silently pleading with him not to go.

He heard her voice in his mind again. "Boris, don't be a hero." How many times had she said that to him? At first, it was said in the laughing, joking tones of a loving wife secure in the knowledge of her husband's capabilities. After a while it had become their morning joke, part of their regular breakfast regimen. She would start clearing the dishes, he would strap on his gun, she would accompany him to the door, he would kiss her, and she would say, "Boris, don't be a hero." It had been like that for years.

In the last few months, however, the tone had become strained, almost strident. The whole thing had become serious for her when the threats started. She knew he could handle the various vermin, punks, and hoods in town, but when his own people started trying to pressure him, make him quit, fire him, and then frame him out of office, she didn't know what he would do. But because she loved him, she kept silent. Except for those five words. "Boris, don't be a hero."

In the back of his mind, where Boris filed everything he didn't need for his work, he realized that she understood, but because of all the pressure, he found himself taking his frustration out on her. All of a sudden, it was like he couldn't do anything right. She didn't like his drinking, she didn't like his overtime, hell, she didn't even like sex anymore. He thought this little vacation would smooth things out. Sure, a little time away, let the whole thing blow over, let Nash take care of everything—that would satisfy her.

And she was just beginning to relax when Boopsie bought it. Now Boris Tucker saw what his wife was thinking written all over her face.

Leave it alone. Put the gun away. We weren't hurt. Let the locals handle it.

But she didn't realize what he did. She didn't have the experience to know that the hole in the cartoon character's head couldn't have been made with anything but a high-powered handgun shot at close range with a silencer. And anyone shooting a high-powered handgun with a silencer was after blood. And the only important blood Boris Tucker knew of in the immediate vicinity was Boris Tucker's. And he wasn't about to let his own assassin get away.

When the milling, curious crowd got a glimpse of Tucker's high-luster blue Bulldog revolver gripped in his meaty hand, they gave the sheriff plenty of room. He pushed through like a maddened bull, his head down, his beady eyes darting from side to side.

He saw the dusty yellow road of the amusement park swirling from the many vacationers' feet. He saw the worn wooden plankings that made up the vaguely wild West buildings on both sides of the street. He saw the faces of the parks' employees. Those who knew about Boopsie looked shocked. Those who didn't, looked tired. There was not one security guard, shocked or tired, to be seen.

That's what I get for being too cheap to go to Disneyland, Tucker thought, still moving purposely forward. If anything untoward happened in the world of Mickey Mouse, there would be dozens of smiling, short-haired gentlemen with twenty-five inch biceps crawling all over the place within seconds. But here, at the Fullerton, California, "Western Ghost Town," where the sound of stuntmen shooting blanks at each other occurred all day long, the Boopsie attack could go ignored for minutes.

It just goes to show, Tucker told himself, you've got to do everything yourself. You can't trust anyone to protect you. The educational and judicial systems in the country had shown themselves to be hollow. Tucker had to admit that even the enforcement branches of the United States were ineffectual shells of what they had been. The whole thing was criminal-oriented, not victim-oriented. If the law had its way, he wouldn't have even been carrying his Bulldog and the assassin could have mowed them all down.

But no one was going to tell Boris Tucker where and when he could carry his own weapon. The Bulldog was a good, solid, inexpensive .44-caliber revolver, perfect for personal use It was about four inches shorter and twenty-three ounces lighter than the Smith and Wesson .357 Magnum he used on the job. Its five-shot, double-action, and ramp-front sight was good enough for him. And it would be enough to take care of this assassin, he thought. But first, he had to find him.

Tucker had stalked to the end of the street without catching a glimpse of white overalls. But as soon as he came around the right corner, a hunk of wood at least six inches long ripped off the side of a building next to his head and spun behind Tucker's neck.

The sheriff heard a mechanical cough as he instinctively fell to one knee, brought his revolver up with both hands, caught a glimpse of a white-overalled knee, and fired.

Tucker's aim was good. He hit the exact spot the man in the overalls' heart would have been if a tree hadn't been in the way.

Tucker's judgment was bad. As soon as the crackling retort of his revolver echoed through the area, most of the tourists turned toward him, expecting the start of another show. The smiles on their faces disappeared, however, when they saw a husky blond man in a red Hawaiian shirt and beige work pants shooting at a tree with a Bulldog instead of a black-garbed bad guy challenging the marshall with a six shooter. Suddenly most of the families found a pressing need to shop inside or go have lunch.

As Tucker rose to his feet, the street started clearing. Tucker blinked. The man in the overalls was no longer behind the tree. The sheriff walked quickly to its gnarled trunk. Damn, he thought, pushing his finger into the hole his bullet had made, this guy is pretty good. He smiled in spite of himself. In a strange sort of way, he savored the coming confrontation.

Boris Tucker wasn't worried. He had faced every

sort of killer in his eighteen years on the police force. And just because he had become the head man didn't mean he didn't see any street action anymore. Although he had no doubt as to the outcome of this little shoot-out, he appreciated the hitman's hit-and-run technique.

Then the smile faded. No hopped-up asshole who would try to kill a man in front of his family was going to get the better of him. It would be a pleasure to run this bastard to ground.

Tucker scanned the area again. It was the main street of the park; a small green which he was standing in the middle of, surrounded by taverns, general stores, and the like. He placed himself in the position the hitman had been in. Looking over his shoulder, he saw the inviting entrance of an alleyway. That's where the guy must've gone, Tucker was sure of it.

Tucker approached the mouth with a cautious, but steady pace. He wanted to be ready if the hitman was just inside, weapon aimed. He thrust his own gun out before him, then ran in low and fast.

The dirt around his feet shot up like suddenly erupting geysers. The whine of a ricochet sounded by his right ear as he fell, rolled, and came up to a crouch beside some cans. Above him came the sound of a subdued case of the whooping cough. Tucker snapped off two shots in that direction without even looking.

When his eyes did move up, he saw the man in the white overalls moving away from the edge of the roof, pulling his weapon in with him. Tucker wanted to laugh. No wonder the assassin hadn't been able to hit him in three separate tries. By the looks of it, the hitman was using a Magnum revolver. A Magnum of at least a .41 caliber with at least a six and a half inch barrel. And with the silencer attached, the assassin was lugging around a gun that was at least fifteen inches long and weighed at least fifty ounces! It was the biggest of the big cannons. Its range and power were truly awe-inspiring but shooting it was akin to handling a bucking mule.

Tucker knew of only one man who could handle a piece like that with any accuracy and that man wouldn't be trying to kill him. Hell, he was friends with that man.

They were supposed to have dinner together that very night. Tucker shook his head in disbelief. This was going to be even easier than he'd expected. And it would make one hell of a dinner conversation.

Tucker hauled himself up and ran to the back of the alley. With any luck he could cut the assassin off before the bastard made it back to the street. Sure enough, the sheriff saw the man in the white overalls high-tailing it out the back window of the nearest building and across the wooden ceiling of the sidewalk awning.

Tucker thrust his arm up so that it made a line, punctuated by his right eye. He aimed his gun barrel in front of the running man then waited until the assassin started to turn toward him. He held his ground and realigned his aim Just as he pulled the trigger, the man in the white overalls stopped dead in his tracks. The Bulldog cracked and the bullet swept by the hitman, missing him by just a few inches.

Tucker immediately ran forward a few steps. Even though the hitman's gun was huge and awkward, the sheriff was taking no chances at this range. He wanted to get under the cover of the awning.

As soon as he had made it a section of the ceiling blew in, slapping the back of Tucker's neck with wooden splinters. He spat through clenched teeth. He had to hand it to the assassin He was willing to try and nail his target by shooting through planks of solid oak.

Tucker hurled himself against the back wall of the building, his Bulldog held by his side. He wasn't about to give his location away by shooting back and he didn't think the hitman would be stupid enough to look for him through the hole.

He was right. Tucker heard the sound of the man's feet trotting across the awning above him toward the building next door. Focusing his attention there, he hastily jerked open his revolver's chamber and dug into his pocket for some more ammunition. By his count, both of them were down to their last bullet.

The assassin seemed to have the same thought. Tucker heard the footsteps slow and then stop near the edge of the awning. As he pulled out three Remington

240 bullets and slipped them in the chambers, he wondered whether he should chance slamming a shell into the ceiling where he pegged the hitman to be. He decided to save his ammo. There was too much chance of a screwup. Even if he caught him in the foot, leg, or balls, the guy could still be as dangerous as a rattlesnake with its tail cut off. The chance of catching him in a mortal area was slim. Tucker wanted to peg him cleanly and permanently.

The sheriff had just slipped his last round in and swung the chamber shut when the footsteps began anew. Slowly, Tucker began to follow the sounds underneath. Both men stopped at the far end of the awning.

This was it, Tucker reasoned. The assassin either had to retrace his steps or jump off this edge. There seemed to be nowhere else he could go. But as soon as the sheriff finished thinking that, he heard the rasping scrape of a window being opened.

Cursing himself as an overconfident fool, Tucker leaped out from under the awning just in time to see the man in the overalls jumping inside a small, dirty gray window. The sheriff snapped off another shot at the hitman which chopped off a piece of the hitman's rubber heel. Then the guy was gone; safe inside the building.

Tucker was pissed. He ran the length of the building's base, looking for a way inside. Coming to the corner, he took a moment to scan the rest of the street. Like the one he just left, it was dusty and empty. Whether it was that way because of the gunfight or general tourist apathy he wasn't sure.

There was no door on the back wall. Tucker stuck his head and weapon around the corner. Another alleyway, also empty. But there, directly in the center of the side wall, was a plain wooden door secured with a Yale lock.

Tucker looked up. The only place the hitman could pick him off from was a single window, which was painted over and closed. And there was no way Tucker could see him getting it open without plenty of warning.

So deciding, the sheriff moved down the alley, stuck

the barrel of his gun two inches from the lock and shot it off. Just as the lead bit through the steel tubing, Tucker threw the broken lock aside and hurled all 240 pounds of himself against the door. It smashed inward, whole planks cracking from the strain.

Tucker dropped, rolled a little bit, and came up with his gun at the ready. But his only target was a creaking network of metal. Tucker quickly shuffled to the side and leaned up against the back wall. He kept his eyes wide open and staring upward. Within seconds his pupils had adapted to the dank darkness of the interior.

Tucker recognized the machinery as the workings of one of the Ghost Town's rides. Interspersed between the tacky snack bars and the ridiculously overpriced souvenir shops were sideshow attractions. Although most of them were penny arcades outfitted with old pinball machines that still cost a quarter for three balls, occasionally there was the refitted roller coaster and funhouse, of which this was the latter.

Another point notched up for the hitman, Tucker acknowledged If he was to get hunted anywhere, this would be the best place for it. Lots of turns, plenty of places to hide and thin, no-exit hallways. Damn, this guy was good!

Still Tucker refused to worry. Even in such claustrophobic surroundings, a Magnum was a Magnum. Unless the gunman had hand and wrist muscles worthy of an Atlas, he might even miss a target four feet in front of him. The sheriff would have no such problem with his Bulldog. His .44 bullets went where he told them to.

The sheriff's grin stretched into a tight smile that was anything but humorous. He felt his blood pounding through his veins, giving him a high he hadn't felt since the early days on the force. The fifties were good years. That was the last decade the police could do no wrong.

Tucker gathered himself up and moved toward the stairway on the other side of the building. It was a steel construction, more suited as a fire escape than an amusement park catwalk. But one good thing about its slat construction was that you could see right up it, all the way to the top. No one could hide on it. It was the landings and what they attached to that Tucker had to worry about.

Just as the sheriff moved up the first flight, he heard a door opening above. He looked up in time to see the second-floor door closing. He leaped up the remaining steps two at a time. But instead of barging through the door, firing his gun like a madman, Tucker pressed his body to the wall next to the door and then turned the knob slowly. Once he heard the click of the bolt, he tip-toed across the landing to the stairs up to the third floor.

What he hoped would happen did. The building was so old it had settled, making every floor rest unevenly, And the door was so old that the jam was slightly rusted. Given enough time the door would creak open of its own free will. But Boris Tucker would not be behind it. No, Boris Tucker would be on the third floor, looking down, waiting for the hitman to start shooting.

Even with his girth, Tucker moved up the stairs silently and smoothly. He placed his hand on the knob, turned, and swung the door open. Then the world blew up in his face.

All he saw was a fuzzy band of white intersperced with ribbons of yellow, orange and red. He felt a searing heat rip across his face and the door tear out of his hand. He heard a cough mingled in with a smashing, whoomping sound. A dozen wooden needles dug into the back of his head as he fell over.

On the way down he realized what had happened. The bastard had been one step ahead of him all along. He had opened the second floor door knowing that Tucker would move up to the third, then, somehow, he had gotten to the third floor himself and waited for him.

After Tucker's mind had pieced that mystery together, it realized two more things. First, he wasn't dead. Second, if he was going to stay that way, he'd better start fighting back.

Even as Tucker slammed to the floor on his left side, his right arm was holding his gun out and his trigger finger was contracting spasmodically.

He knew his bullets had missed even before his

vision cleared. He heard them whine off in several directions and the hasty footsteps of the hitman receding in the distance. When the rainbow haze finally dissipated he saw why it was so easy for the assassin to change floors. Now he was lying on a catwalk. A catwalk that stretched from one door to another. All around him were the workings of the ride. Turning rods, twisting valves, spiraling hooks, all were working their mechanical magic around him.

Tucker painfully rose to a sitting position. He felt a warmth covering the entire right side of his face. When he touched it and brought his hand away, he saw his palm covered with blood. The hitman's bullet had just creased his cheek, Tucker realized. But that graze was enough to hack out a canal of flesh from the side of his nose to his ear. If the bullet had been even a fraction of an inch farther to the left, Tucker's head would have split and disintegrated like a rotten melon. High-powered Magnums may not be that easy to control, but when they hit something, that's it for that something.

Enraged by the assassin and his own stupidity, Tucker emptied his remaining bullets into the door at the other end of the catwalk. To his shock, he heard a high-pitched scream in reply. Not the sort of sound one might attribute to a hardened hitman. More like the sound a frightened young girl would make.

The realization brought Tucker to his feet. He had just fired into an amusement park ride filled with innocent tourists.

With grim determination, Tucker reloaded his weapon a second time. He refused to consider that the hitman was smarter than he was. Luck of the draw, that's all it was. The ignorant bastard was merely taking advantage of some lucky breaks. This creep would even use innocent vacationers as a shield. It would be Tucker's pleasure to blow his brains out.

Swinging his chamber shut again, Tucker marched to the second door and kicked it open. Standing directly in front of him was a man with a gun. The man with the gun started to aim his weapon in Tucker's direction. With great satisfaction Tucker shot the figure twice in the chest.

A light went on above the figure reading "YOU WON."

It was then Tucker realized that he had beaten a mechanical dummy to the draw. The dummy started spitting sparks from his wounds. Standing to the side was a young girl with both hands in her mouth. Standing next to her was a young man with both arms around her. All four of their eyes were wide and staring at Tucker.

The sheriff felt like a first-class fool. He lowered his gun, looked around, then returned his attention to the kids.

"You see another guy with a gun come out of there?" he asked, pointing a thumb at the open door.

The kids kept staring.

"A big guy," Tucker continued. "Dark hair, wearing white overalls?"

The kids stared for another second, then turned and ran.

"Hey!" Tucker called after them. "Hey! I'm not gonna hurt you! Hey, wait a minute!"

The sheriff started off after them, keeping an eye out for the hitman. He was striding across a black floor surrounded by black walls and a black ceiling. The environment gave the effect of the Twilight Zone. Tucker couldn't be sure in which direction he was actually heading. He had let the hitman lead him into the Ghost Town's Funhouse.

He saw the kids turn a corner and followed. He stepped into the entrance for the Hall of Mirrors. The kids had already entered and were stumbling through, slamming into glass partitions every few seconds.

Tucker saw his own reflection. No wonder the kids had reacted so strongly. In his haste and rage, the sheriff had forgotten about his wound. Not only had he shot a harmless dummy, he had blood dribbling across the bottom of his head. Well, there was nothing he could do about it now, he thought. The Hall of Mirrors was the last attraction the Funhouse had to offer, he remembered from the brochures. Once patrons got through that, the literature said, they would be treated to a wild ride and then out.

Tucker had no interest in the exit. There was still a mad-dog assassin to catch. He was about to turn back when a fourth reflection appeared in the hall. It was the reflection of the mad-dog assassin.

It was Tucker's first good look at the man. The body filled out the dirty white overalls, showing signs of a solid musculature beneath. The face was wide, his eyes were gray and widely set, and the mouth was thin and wide. The only thing marring the expanse were pock-marked acne scars across both cheeks. The hitman could be called handsome in a very rough sort of way, but none of the three present were pleased at his appearance. Especially since he held his huge revolver up in plain view.

Without hesitation, Tucker raised his own gun, took aim and fired. A spider-web seemed to hang by itself in the space directly in front of the sheriff as several mirrors beyond that shattered and collapsed. Beyond those mirrors was a blank gray wall. Tucker had misjudged the situation again, losing a bullet in the process. And here was no place to hide and reload.

The hitman's reflection was no longer in front of him. Tucker spun until he spied the white overalls moving behind him. The sheriff's lips drew back from his teeth as a wolf's might. The assassin had taken a gamble. Here no one could be sure where anyone else actually was. And here, once all one's bullets were used, the other could blast away until most of the mirrors were gone. Then it would be a race to see who could reload fast enough.

At least there was a way to tell the actual reflections from the plain transparent wall sheets. The transparent partitions were made of Plexiglas, plastic, and didn't shatter when shot. They created the impression of hovering spiderwebs. And it was the hitman's turn to make holes in them. Tucker had expended three of his five bullets getting to this point. The hitman could have reloaded right after he shot the sheriff at the third floor entrance.

So it was a matter of patience and stalking now. It was a matter of who would break first, the hitman, Tucker, or the two young kids stuck in the middle. The girl had started shrieking the second after Tucker had shot through the glass, and she had continued shrieking no matter how her boyfriend tried to soothe her. Finally it became a matter of shutting her up. The boy pulled her hands away from her face, wrapped one of his arms around her waist and pushed his other hand over her mouth.

"Candy," he said, "take it easy. Just keep quiet and lie down here, OK? Just keep your head down and your fingers in your ears. I'm going to try to find the exit and get help."

He half-lowered, half-pushed her to the floor as the two armed men began to move slowly around the hall. Then the boy, too, began to move. Tucker was about to yell to the kid to get down himself, but he cut off the words just as they were gathering behind his lips. When the boy had spoken, the sheriff had been able to pinpoint his location instantly. He could've shot the kid with no problem at all. If he spoke, it was quite possible that the hitman could return the favor. Boris Tucker kept quiet and kept stalking. The other two men did the same.

The dance around the Hall of Mirrors was excruciatingly slow. Each man did his best to keep the other in view and not knock embarrassingly against the clear partitions. The hitman and Tucker kept their free arms held out in front of them, but the kid was so desperate he would often smack face first against the clear plastic.

Tucker began to sweat profusely. He told himself he wasn't worried, but he also told himself that he'd have to be lucky in this environment. He'd have to nail the hitman dead to rights or he'd make himself a sitting duck. A sudden haze swept across his brain. His view got slightly orange at the edges for a second. It must be the wound, he thought. The loss of blood might be weakening him.

The loss of blood . . . ?

When it happened, it happened very fast. Tucker looked down and saw the red splotches he had been dotting the floor with since his entry into the Funhouse. He realized that the hitman could follow those splotches directly to him. He realized that the reflection of the hitman in front of him was coming from behind him. He

21

spun in his tracks and fired his remaining bullets back the way he had come.

The Hall of Mirrors was filled with the sounds of breaking glass, gun reports, Candy's cries, and Tucker's curses.

The sheriff fell down, digging into his ammo pocket before he hit the floorboards. The hitman's bullets began digging into the floorboards before Tucker had shoved his hand all the way in. Taking no chances, the sheriff simply turned his pocket inside out and clawed at whatever ammunition was rolling around.

Tucker had just filled his second chamber when a bullet splattered into the ground by his nose. That was it, he thought. The assassin had the proper range. The next bullet would lodge somewhere in him. The sheriff slammed his revolver shut and raised his arm to protect himself. So it was that he saw the hitman change his target.

The man in the overalls leveled his weapon at eye level and blasted twice off to Tucker's right. Glass shattered to Tucker's left. The wounded lawman rolled over to see the broken reflectors reveal the stunned young man. The kid tried to leap through a Plexiglas partition, only to be thrown back. He tried to run away, but a mirror was blocking his path. He was about to hurl himself to the side when the assassin shot him in the back.

The marksmanship was impeccable. The hitman used both hands and, with calm assurance, killed the boy in cold blood.

Candy wailed in shock and despair, rolling back and forth between plastic partitions.

"Had to die," the man in the overalls quietly said as the last echo of his coughing report disappeared. "He was getting too close to the exit. Knew what I looked like. Couldn't let him get away. Sorry."

Tucker listened in angry awe. Then he said, "Bastard!" and fired his newly loaded rounds.

The hitman was forced to duck as the sheriff's bullets smashed glass all around him. The lawman had been right. It was very easy to place a talking target. He was

22

also right about the race to reload. Now both men had empty guns. The hitman scuttled to the right and around the hysterical girl as he pulled his plastic speed loaders from an overall pocket. Within seconds, six new shells were in the silenced Magnum.

In the same amount of time, Tucker had only been able to find and load three of his rounds. He had spotted another lying next to his stomach when the hitman opened fire again. Tucker stayed cool and listened. Amidst all the breaking glass he heard the cough of the silencer coming from just left of the boy's body.

He looked up to see the hitman reflected behind him. In front of him was the boy's body. Tucker stood and fired above the corpse. Mirrors were mowed down in succession, revealing the man in the overalls. Tucker fired again. The hitman disappeared.

Tucker thought about it for only a second. The assassin had said the boy was getting near the exit. The brochure had said the exit started with a wild ride. It meant that the hitman had found the exit and fallen down it. If Tucker could catch him off guard, he'd be able to kill him with his last bullet.

With a roar, Tucker folded both arms in front of his face and charged. He felt the plastic partitions fold before him as he smashed his way toward the young man's corpse. He kicked the remaining shards of mirror out of the way as the last few feet were covered. Below his folded arms, he saw the exit was a gently sloping trap door. And before he could do anything about it, he saw the man in the white overalls propped just under the trap door.

The man in the white overalls shot Boris Tucker in the chin. The bullet came out of the sheriff's hair, taking most of his head with it.

Minutes before, the noise of the gun battle had attracted a large crowd outside of the Funhouse exit. So Mrs. Tucker was there with her daughter when what was left of her husband came rolling out.

Two

San Francisco Homicide Inspector Harry Callahan stepped out of his rented Cordoba and scowled. He didn't like the attitude of the officer who stopped him at the amusement park gate. He didn't like the looks of the place. He didn't like the way the sun was shining. It was shaping up to be one lousy visit.

He looked over to where a huge, blue-uniformed crowd had gathered around the front of the Ghost Town Funhouse. Pencils were hurriedly scribbling and flashbulbs were going off in the middle of the afternoon. Harry couldn't see anything else besides the sea of blue.

"Is that . . . ?" said a voice from over his left shoulder. He turned around. "It is!" said one of two men beneath a gnarled tree in the center of a little green. "Dirty Harry Callahan, as I live and breath. How the hell did you get here, Callahan?"

Harry slowly took off his sunglasses and recognized Lieutenant Fritz Williamson of the Fullerton homicide squad. There weren't many cops in the Southern California area Harry didn't know and there were even fewer who didn't know him. Many departments were often put on standby alert when a police chief heard Dirty Harry was in town. It seemed as if Fullerton hadn't gotten the word.

"Well, I took the Santa Ana Freeway to Riverside . . ." Harry said softly without a smile.

Williamson laughed in spite of that, coming over to the car. Harry remembered the lieutenant as a nice enough guy, but a little slow on the uptake.

"Yeah, right," Williamson waved Harry's directions away. "Well, what the hell are you doing here then?"

Harry turned back to look at the scurrying cops in front of the Funhouse. "I had a dinner engagement," he said, slipping his sunglasses back on.

"So?" Williamson replied. "It's in the middle of the afternoon."

The lieutenant was living up to his reputation. "My date is in no shape to chew food," Harry said pointedly.

"All right, I'll bite," Williamson retorted affably. "Why is your date in no shape to chew food?"

Harry sighed, then answered in a flat tone. "Because he's missing half his head."

Williamson finally got it. "Half his hea . . . oh jeez, Harry, I'm sorry. Really, I had no idea."

"That's OK, Fritz," Harry said. He shook his head. No wonder his men called him "On the Fritz," behind his back. "What happened here?"

"How much do you know, Harry?" Williamson asked as he came around the car, motioning his associate to follow.

"Only as much as the police radio band and CB scuttlebutt said. Murder at the amusement park. Fellow officer shot in the line of duty. The usual. Boris said he might be taking Dotty and Lynn here this afternoon. I put two and two together."

"Christ," Williamson shoved his hands in his pockets and looked at his shoes. "The truckers must've really gotten off on it, huh?"

"Yeah," said Harry. "A lot of excited talk about calibers and what looked like rotten melons."

26

"Christ," Williamson said again. "Come on."

The two men moved toward the Funhouse entrance. As they walked up the steps Harry noticed a dark splotch just under the exit sign to his right.

"It really stinks," he heard Williamson say. "We found him there. Most of the gore dropped out on the way down."

Harry turned toward the Fullerton cop. "Did Dotty see him?"

"Yeah."

"Where is she?"

"Around the back. With Sergeant Baker."

Harry moved purposely past the dark bloodstain on the yellow dust and walked around the corner. Just as he turned he heard Williamson mutter to his aide, "Jesus. I didn't know he had any friends." Well, not anymore. Harry's definition of a friend was someone he didn't know from his immediate job that he was willing to go and see. Otherwise he kept up a friendly banter with the guys at work and let the girls come to him when they both found time.

If Boris Tucker wasn't the last of the out-of-state associates, Harry would have a hard time figuring out who was. He sure wouldn't cross the street for Fritz Williamson. As a matter of fact, ever since he'd met both Williamson and Tucker at a Midwest crime seminar he was forced to attend by his superiors, Harry knew that the latter man would make a good partner and a great beer-drinking buddy. It was too bad he toiled away in San Antonio, Texas, as a sheriff, and wasn't willing to make the hop into Harry's San Francisco suicide seat.

His wife and kid probably had something to do with it. Dotty was a good cop's wife, one of the best. Her father had been a politician and a bad one at that. He was part of a Texas state machine and was therefore always around and never took a stand on anything that wasn't dictated to him. By the time Boris asked for her hand, she was ready for a strong man who acted on what he believed in.

Look where it got her, Harry thought coming around

the back of the Funhouse, sitting on the back flap of a station wagon sobbing into a paper towel with a plain-clothesman offering her a Styrofoam cup full of coffee.

As soon as she saw him, she was up on her feet and running toward him. Harry caught her in his arms and held her tightly. Her small thin body shook next to his. He felt her bones drift in and out and saw her head bobbing with controlled emotion.

"The bastards," she said. "The bastards. They set it up. They set it all up. He didn't stand a chance."

"Bastards?" asked Harry. "What bastards, Dotty? Who are 'they'?"

"Those—those bastards at his office," the woman choked out. "They did this to him. They did it."

"Come on, Dotty," Harry said, torn between soothing and grilling the crying woman. "Take it easy. You're not making any sense."

"They did it," she repeated, looking up at him. "I swear it, Harry. Nash and all the others."

"Nash . . . ?" Harry began, only to be interrupted by a strong hand gripping his upper arm. He turned and looked down into the face of Sergeant Lee Baker, a wiry, tawny-haired cop.

"You take it easy, Stilt," Baker said. "Can't you see the lady's in bad shape?"

"Go write a report," Harry quietly replied. "I'm a friend of the family."

"I don't care if you're the Pope," Baker snarled. "The lady is in my protective custody and she's in no shape to answer questions."

Harry had to agree with the sergeant there, but he wasn't about to admit it. Instead he lowered his head to look into Mrs. Tucker's tearful eyes.

"I'm sorry, Dotty," he told her. "I'll find out what happened."

The woman stopped crying, then spent several seconds looking at Harry's eyes. Then she nodded. Harry squeezed her arms as a gesture of optimism, then gently led her back to Baker. But before he left, he eyed the sergeant up and down. "No need to be so hostile," Harry told him. "You're not *that* short."

Before Baker could reply, Harry marched back to the front of the Funhouse where Lieutenant Williamson was going over some notes with his aide.

"The kid's got a bad case of grandeur," Harry said.

"Who?" Williamson replied. "Oh, Baker? His bark is worse than his bite."

"You might think about buying him a leash then," Harry answered, glancing at the notes. "What's the bottom line here?"

Williamson waved his aide away, took Harry's arm, and led him inside before answering. "The M.E. figures three dead before too long, including Tucker. The first kid got the top of his head chopped off, but is still alive. But between the shock, blood loss, and wound, we don't figure he's got much of a chance."

Harry had heard enough. "Where's the bastard who did this?" he demanded.

"What?" Williamson replied.

"This, all this," Harry said slowly. "You mean to tell me that with a gunfight raging inside a funhouse and a murdered sheriff, you couldn't catch the bastard who started it?"

"What are you talking about, Harry?" Williamson wanted to know, his expression a mask of confusion.

It took a major effort for Harry to control himself. He blinked, swallowed, and put a hand on Williamson's shoulder. The left side of his upper lip curled off of his teeth when he spoke. And his voice was not much louder than a whisper.

"Fritz, the radio reports said there was a gunfight here. You told me that three people got killed. There's a woman and her child back there who'll never be the same again. And you mean to tell me you let the man who did it get away?"

"Nobody got away," said a strident voice behind Harry. He recognized it even before he turned around. It was the voice of Sergeant Baker.

"I thought you were in protective custody," said Harry.

Baker stepped in between Harry and Williamson, the top of his head getting redder and redder. "Who the hell is this?" he demanded of his superior. "What the hell is he doing in the middle of a Fullerton investigation?"

"This is Harry Callahan," replied Williamson, seemingly relieved by the interruption. "He's an Inspector with the San Francisco Homicide Divi—"

"I've heard of him," Baker interrupted again, returning his attention to Callahan. "So you're Dirty Harry, huh? A lot of people seem to die around you, Stilt."

Harry answered carefully. "A lot of them deserve it."

"Yeah," drawled Baker, smirking. "I'll watch where I stand." He turned back to Williamson. "So what is he doing here, Fritz? We don't need a San Fran dick on a simple murder-suicide."

The surprise in Harry's voice was sharp. "Murder-suicide? What is this?"

"Your buddy-boy started shooting, that's what," Baker snorted. "He only blew his own brains out after blasting two innocent kids."

Harry looked down at the sergeant as if examining a particularly offensive slug. "You're crazy," he told him flatly.

"Harry," Williamson interceded, "Tucker was under a lot of pressure. Dotty herself corroborated this. He was getting old. He was near retirement time. And everybody in the park agreed that he started shooting. We have a dozen eyewitnesses who saw him shoot that tree and wave his gun around."

"Yeah," echoed Baker, "the ballistic boys have already collected lead from everywhere. All the shells were .44 specials." Suddenly Baker's face became the picture of innocence. "Like the gun you use," he continued sweetly. "You didn't happen to be in the area, did you, Callahan?"

"That's enough!" Williamson snapped. "I'm sorry, Harry, but it looks real bad. At the very least Tucker was breaking the law by carrying his weapon over state lines. That's a bad sign."

"Come on, Fritz," Harry growled. "No good cop leaves his piece behind."

"The law says—" Baker began.

"The law says Boris Tucker shot two kids and killed himself," Harry interrupted. "The law says a lot of stupid things."

"Yeah, the law says you're also out of your jurisdiction, Stilt!" Baker yelled. "So get lost!"

"Shut up, Sergeant!" Williamson barked. "Get back to Mrs. Tucker and see that she's all right."

Baker clamped his mouth shut, looked to the lieutenant and then to Harry, then abruptly turned heel and walked away.

"That guy doesn't need a leash," Harry noted, "he needs a muzzle."

"Come on, Harry," Williamson complained. "It's tough enough already."

"Yeah," Harry muttered. "Can I look upstairs, Fritz?"

"Sure, Harry, sure. Our guys have gone over it already. Go ahead."

Harry Callahan wearily marched up the back steps of the Funhouse. He felt the comforting weight of his own .44 Magnum against his side, while thinking about the individuality of each weapon. A bullet fired from his gun would look entirely different from the same sort of round fired from Tucker's Bulldog. But only under a microscope. And the way the Fullerton force was playing it, Harry doubted the investigation would go that far.

An aging cop under a lot of pressure goes beserk, then kills himself. It's happened before. Neat and tidy. Only Harry knew Tucker didn't do it. He was the kind of man who might kill himself all right, but he wouldn't have taken anybody with him.

Harry stopped in front of the third floor door with the ragged hole in it. Shot from the outside, Harry realized. He put his hand on the doorknob, then took it off again. Instead of walking through to the Hall of Mirrors, Harry kneeled down on the metal staircase. He looked carefully at the steel slats. Suddenly he rose and checked the wall behind him. It was flat, unscarred by holes.

Starting from the wall, Harry traced the length of

31

each steel slat with his eyes. He had traced six when he found what he was looking for. Wedged in between two of the flat metal lengths was a squashed slug. It was the bullet that had punched the hole in the wooden door. Its velocity must have been slowed down enough by that so the lead didn't sink into the wall but got caught by the metal. And it wouldn't have been found if someone wasn't looking specifically for it.

Harry slipped the slug into his jacket pocket and went to check the Hall of Mirrors. The place, not surprisingly, was a wreck. Most of the mirrors were destroyed so that the hall was made up of a maze of bullet-ridden Plexiglas sheets. Harry walked amid them, looking at his shoes. Halfway around the right side, he saw something amid the shattered mirror shards. He reached down and picked it up. It was a button. A square, light-green button.

He checked out the rest of the area. He found eleven cents worth of change, two cigarette stubs, and six entry ticket stubs. Harry kept the change and the tickets. They joined the slug and the button in his pocket. Then he retraced his steps and went back downstairs.

"Find anything?" Williamson asked.

"Nope," Harry replied.

"Where are those reports?" shouted Lieutenant Al Bressler out the open door of his office.

"Which reports?" asked Sergeant Reineke from his desk.

"The reports . . . you know the reports," Bressler sputtered, waving his arms in little circular motions over his desk.

"The ones on the Kleindale Jewelry heist?" asked Reineke. The lieutenant shook his head. "The Allegra shooting?" Bressler shook his head again. "The Wilson stabbing?"

"No, you know . . . come on . . . the ones about the suicide thing . . . in Texas."

"Oh yeah, the Tucker case," acknowledged Reineke. "Harry's got 'em."

Bressler threw his hands up and stormed out of his office. He quickly walked in between the sergeants' desks and moved down the man-made hallway toward the inspectors' offices.

The world may keep turning, Bressler thought as he marched past different squad rooms, but some things never change. Like the San Francisco homicide office. It was still on the seventh floor of the Justice Building, it was still in suite #750 and, no matter how they changed the desks or how many partitions they moved in, the ambience stayed the same. Too much smoke, too many junk food wrappers, and too big a stink from Vitalis, Right Guard. and bad booze. The custodians try, God love them. but they only make the offices smell like the inside of a Band-Aid two days after.

Bressler came to Harry's office cubicle and stuck his head in. The only one there was Frank DiGeorgio, who was reading a 1977 issue of *Playboy*.

"Where's Callahan?" the lieutenant asked.

DiGeorgio jerked in his chair, the magazine nearly hopping out of his hands. When he saw it was Bressler doing the asking. he swallowed the curse that leaped to his lips and collected himself. "Down in Missing Persons, I think," was what he finally said.

Bressler nodded. "Good article?" he asked before he left.

"Article?" DiGeorgio replied. "Oh yeah. Right. Good article."

The lieutenant should've chewed DiGeorgio out, and he would have if it had been anyone else, but being Harry Callahan's partner was dangerous enough. That was something else that never changed. DiGeorgio was the only one out of six partners to last more than one case. That's why they called Callahan duty the "suicide seat." Only DiGeorgio seemed to have the sense and the timing to get out of Harry's way when he played superhero.

It was Harry himself who always seemed to need the chewing out. That was the only way Bressler knew of controlling him. besides giving him plenty of rope and hoping he didn't choke on it.

After all Harry's tragedies, Bressler mused, it was amazing Harry could be controlled at all. First his wife was killed in a meaningless traffic accident, then there was the "Scorpio" affair where Harry threw away his badge, and recently that terrorist fiasco where DiGeorgio was stabbed and Harry lost his fifth partner; a woman.

And through it all, Harry just kept getting better and better and more and more professional. The "Vigilante Cop" mess probably had something to do with that, Bressler figured. Callahan really had to examine his M.O. during that case.

So now, if anything, Harry was even more devastating in the field. It was just a matter of utilizing him properly. After all their years together, Bressler considered himself the Callahan expert. Unfortunately the various captains, commissioners, and mayors that came and went couldn't claim the same.

Bressler hopped into the elevator and rode down to the fourth floor. He found Harry in suite #436, sitting in Ron Caputo's seat while Ron stood by, staring over Callahan's shoulder.

"What are you doing, Harry?" Bressler boomed, a grin on his face, "Bucking for a transfer? Harry Callahan, tracer of lost persons. That has a nice ring to it."

Harry said nothing, just grimaced and kept reading the papers in front of him. Ron looked at the lieutenant, smiled and shrugged, as if saying, "Harry's at it again." When Callahan got worked up over something, the office crew stayed out of his way.

"Come on, Harry," continued Bressler, moving over to the other side of the desk, "what are you doing? It wouldn't have anything to do with homicide, would it? After all, that is the department you're supposed to be assigned to. And God knows there are enough murders to go around."

"Just checking something," Harry grunted without looking up.

Bressler looked under Callahan's arm and read a piece of the report Harry was so intent on. "—therefore I see no reason why any further investigation into Tucker's death is warranted—"

"All right, Callahan, that's it!" Bressler exploded, pulling the papers out from under his gaze. Harry was immediately on his feet, facing the lieutenant like baseball manager Billy Martin after a particularly bad umpire call. Bressler cut him off before he could complain. "Now you're bucking for a demotion," he said. "These are private files, lieutenant to lieutenant. That's bad enough, but wasting time with a suicide when the workload is incredible—"

"It was no suicide," said Harry.

Bressler took a sympathetic tact. "Look, Harry, I know you liked the guy. Hell, we all did, but that's the way it goes sometimes. Leave it be. Believe me, it'll go away."

"Lieutenant . . ." Harry began.

"Get your mind off it, Harry," Bressler continued. "DiGeorgio is waiting upstairs. We've got to get a break on this Fullmer rape-murder thing."

"All right, Lieutenant," said Harry. "Come on."

The two men stomped out of Caputo's office with a cursory wave. The Missing Persons' officer gave Harry the thumb's-up sign. Just as he was rounding the bend, Harry gave him back an "A-OK." Bressler kept his head down and headed for the elevators. Harry kept going past them.

"Hey!" Bressler called after him. "Where are you going?"

"To ballistics," Harry replied, still moving.

"What for?" Bressler shouted.

"To show you something," Harry answered. "Want to come?"

Bressler followed, cursing all the way. Walter White, the homicide lab man, was waiting for them.

"I see you got him here, Harry," he said. "What did you do, promise him a cookie?"

"No lip, White," Bressler warned. The lieutenant only enjoyed the lab man's Don Rickles impersonation after hours. "What is this about?"

"Boris Tucker," Harry said.

"Boris Tucker shot himself," Bressler declared flatly.

"Boris Tucker," Harry repeated, "was murdered in cold blood. So were the two kids who died with him. And there's a good possibility that there's a fourth victim."

Bressler was unimpressed. "Funny I missed your deerstalker when I walked in, Sherlock. You bucking for vacation time?"

In way of reply, Harry walked over to a white drawer, pulled it open, took out a large manila envelope, came back to where Bressler was standing, opened it, and dumped the contents onto the lab counter.

"Very impressive," Bressler drawled. "A flattened slug, a ticket stub, a hunk of rubber, and a pretty green button. So what?"

"So this," Harry said, picking up the squashed bullet. "Walter just gave me the report on this. It is a totally different filing than any bullet shot from Tucker's Bulldog revolver."

"Where did you get that?" Bressler said dangerously.

Harry dropped his arm to his side and looked at the lieutenant with veiled eyelids. "A pigeon dropped it on me," he answered.

"Christ, Harry! Jesus Christ! Withholding evidence on a Fullerton investigation? You know what could happen?"

"Aw, come on, Lieutenant, you know those guys wouldn't have bothered checking this far."

"It makes no difference, and you know it, Callahan! You could be brought up on charges."

"No way," said Harry.

"How do you figure?" Bressler asked, getting intrigued. There was always a method to Harry's madness.

"Because it's not just a Fullerton investigation anymore," Harry explained, holding up the hunk of rubber. "I found this on the back awning of the Ghost Town Funhouse, near another bullet hole. I was told it was a piece from a shoe heel." Harry used the rubber like a magic marker and smeared a black line across the lab counter with it.

"Oh hell, Harry, I'm going to have to clean that off," White moaned.

Callahan ignored the joker. "This matches with the same kind of streaks I found in the Hall of Mirrors. Both Tucker and the kid were wearing sneakers. They couldn't have made these marks."

"So?" inquired the lieutenant. "What does that prove? Those marks could have been made any time."

"No way," Harry said again, holding up the ticket stub. "First of all, I checked. The Funhouse is cleaned every night by a nice old guy named Whitney. He's about the only decent employee that place has got. Everything is swept out and washed. He would have noticed the black heel marks if they had been there the day before. And the tickets are dated. The only stubs in there were marked with the day Tucker was killed."

"OK, I grant you," mused Bressler, "you had some overlooked clues to go on. But that's all! All you've done is establish that a man who might have been on the awning was also in the Hall of Mirrors. What good does that do? This guy could have been in the Funhouse at any time of the day. There's no way to establish he was inside when Tucker was."

Harry held up the square green button as if it were a tape-recorded confession.

"Yeah, it's very pretty, Callahan," Bressler said with sarcasm. "Quit savoring the moment and speak."

"Tucker was wearing a Hawaiian shirt with round red buttons. The murdered boy was wearing a gray-striped buttondown with round white ones. I've checked around. Square buttons aren't used very much and the ones that are are usually on women's short sleeve fashion blouses. You know, the silky ones with thin collars."

"What are you telling me?" Bressler inquired. "A hitman with black heels and a green silk shirt?"

"No. Another victim. A missing girl."

"Come on, Harry, this is ridiculous! That button could have been lost any time of the day as well! You're not going to get time off from the Fullmer thing because of a bunch of strung-up assumptions! Facts, I need facts!"

37

Harry Callahan pulled himself up to his full height and moved right up to Bressler, leaving all the Fullerton items behind. "Facts?" he snarled into the lieutenant's forehead. "OK, fact one; the dead kid was named George Garris. Fact two; his mother said he was on a weekend trip with a friend. Fact three; one of his best friends was a girl named Candice McCarthy. Fact four; Candice McCarthy has just been reported missing."

Bressler stared angrily at Harry for five full seconds. Then he said, "Aw, damn."

"The bastard who murdered Boris Tucker is out there," Harry warned. "And he's got a pretty young girl with him."

"OK, Harry, OK," Bressler sighed. "You made your point. It's a string of coincidences, but it's a mighty strong one. I'll call Williamson back and have him put the girl's disappearance on his highest priority."

"No way," Harry said for a third time. "It's my business now."

Bressler was about to bark Harry's head off until he saw the look in the inspector's eye. Instead, he pursed his lips and waited.

"You want to hear another coincidence, lieutenant?" Harry finally asked as he was walking toward the door. "Guess where Candice McCarthy lives? Guess who has jurisdiction?" Without answering, Harry left the lab and went back upstairs to collect DiGeorgio and hit the streets.

Bressler looked at White, who was scrubbing the black heel mark with a wet paper towel while whistling. The lieutenant recognized the tune. It was "I Left My Heart in San Francisco."

"Hockey puck," the lieutenant said.

Three

"Got any ideas, Harry?" asked DiGeorgio.

"About what?" Harry asked back, taking a turn at Green and Kearney streets.

"You've got your choice," DiGeorgio replied, looking out the window at the night life around North Beach. "The Tucker thing, the Fullmer thing, or dinner."

"Dinner," Harry said without hesitation.

"That's what I like about you, Harry," his partner commented. "You're the only one who thinks about his stomach as much as I do."

"I'm tall," Harry explained, taking Grant Avenue around Telegraph Hill. "Besides we've got some time. The whole day's been a bust."

"What've you got in mind?"

"I know a little place on Columbus Avenue. Off the Embarcadero. The atmosphere's a little loud, but the roast beef sandwiches are good. And the onion rings are fried in beer."

"Little place," said DiGeorgio. "Little loud. Roast beef. Onion rings. Beer. Right. I'm with you, Harry."

39

"You better believe it," said Harry.

Tanya's was exactly like Harry described it. The two cops walked right into the midst of an undulating crowd. People were everywhere. To their left was a rectangular dance floor bracketed by a bar along the side wall and a tiny disc jockey's room along the back wall. To their right were six tables set for four and a smaller bar so that the eaters wouldn't have to dig through the dancers to get drinks. This section had a couple of opaque windows lining the side wall and three doors in the rear section.

Harry shouldered his way into the dining area, walking right into the arms of an incredible brunette dressed in a strapless elastic top and designer jeans.

"Harry!" the girl shouted in surprise over the throbbing music. "I thought you said you'd never come back here!"

"I couldn't stay away from the meat," Harry shouted back.

The girl threw her head back and laughed, giving DiGeorgio an enviable view of her torso. Harry wrapped one arm around her back so she wouldn't pop out of her tube top entirely. "Tanya," he called to the girl, "I want you to meet my partner, Frank DiGeorgio. Frank, this is the owner."

"Hey," the girl said, dark eyes sparkling under her lustrous bangs, "good to meet you, Frank. Just sit down boys and enjoy the show. The meat is on me."

She winked at Harry who patted her on the butt as she drifted back toward the kitchen. The two men settled in at the table on the side wall closest to the rest room. DiGeorgio immediately did as Tanya instructed and feasted his eyes on the female dancers. Harry stuck his chin in one hand and looked over the bobbing heads.

The day had indeed been a bust, he recalled. Neither the Garris or McCarthy mothers could tell them anything substantial to go on. The central files weren't much help either. Ever since the Son of Sam massacre, the .44 Magnum had become the favorite weapon of psychos everywhere. Whenever some nut wanted to blow off a little steam by blowing away a few innocents, they cried for their daddy to buy them a Magnum. But there was nothing consistent in the research. Harry couldn't establish a solid link to any particular person.

Harry began to think he was wasting his time in San Fran. It was doubtful the McCarthy girl had been kidnapped back to her place of origin and the key to Tucker's offing certainly wasn't in the City by the Bay. But he couldn't leave the Fullmer thing in Bressler and DiGeorgio's lap. Especially since he was the one who had found the girl in the first place.

Megan Fullmer was a nice, sandy-blonde girl of seventeen. She was found in what was left of a fashion leotard under the Oakland Bay Bridge—just a few blocks away from Tanya's. The department had gotten a few investigatory nibbles, but no solid bites. A couple of other rape-murders cropped up in the North Beach area, but there was no solid connection between them other than the fact that each of the victims should have known better.

That is, either the murdered girls were experienced or on a date. According to all the reports, every single victim wouldn't have accepted a dance with another guy, let alone a ride. There seemed to be no way the murderer could get his target alone.

"Man! You really know how to pick the restaurants!" DiGeorgio shouted to him, taking his mind off the murder musing. Harry smiled in a preoccupied sort of way and followed his partner's gaze. Undulating under a strobe was an attractive auburn-haired girl. She was wearing a silky blue maillot bathing suit with a matching slit skirt and, of all things, a pair of sneakers.

Harry shook his head in wonder. All you need to get into a dance club nowadays, he thought, was a bathing suit and a towel. The girl seemed refreshingly unaffected, so Harry kept a pleased eye on her. The strobe turned off and a multicolored spot turned on, bathing the girl in a rainbow. The girl smiled in appreciation and leaned over to say something to the girl next to her.

The female companion was dressed in a strapless top that had a half-purple, half-blue band across her small breasts and a red torso which was tucked into red latex pants. Her hair was cut short in the shaggy punk style, her eyes were narrow, and her chin was strong and wide. DiGeorgio noticed her, too.

"Dyke city for sure," he commented. Harry just stared at the two girls while blowing on his left hand. The music stopped just as Tanya came back with their sandwiches. She bent down for Harry's benefit, but he was looking over her shoulder at the other girls. He saw the short-hair say something and point to the rest room door. The auburn nodded and said something to her collegiate-looking date. He answered and she turned. Harry saw what she didn't. Just before short-hair followed her, she locked eyes with collegiate. He smiled.

Harry heard a buzzing in his ears. "What?" he said.

"I said," Tanya repeated, "you must have a bad case of dance fever. You're not appreciating the sandwich or me."

Harry kissed her quickly. "Sorry. Got to go to the bathroom. Too much beer." He slid out of his chair and moved toward the back door.

"Is he kidding?" Tanya asked DiGeorgio. DiGeorgio shrugged.

Harry stuck his head around the rest room door. He saw a stairway leading down. He took it to a short hallway going off in two directions, left and right. Down to the left was the ladies' room. To the right was the men's. Harry walked silently to the left and took up a position next to the lavatory door. He looked and listened.

There was no other door in the left part of the hallway, but he heard a strange creaking, as if someone was having trouble with a particularly rusty pipe. Harry put the flat of his hand on the ladies' room door. He leaned in. The door opened a crack. He was about to look when something slapped into the small of his back.

He turned to face a muscle-bound guy with a mustache. "Hey, creep," the guy said, "get your jollies somewhere else."

"I'm a police officer," Harry said with a scowl.

"Yeah, *I'm* Fran Tarkenton and *That's Incredible.*

Hit the road, Tom." The guy jerked a thumb at the stairway, then folded his arms to show off his biceps.

Harry looked at the guy for a second, figured "forget it," then brushed around, and went back upstairs. He remembered what an old partner had said to him after he had been beaten up as a Peeping Tom during the "Scorpio" case. "Maybe that's why they call you Dirty Harry," Chico had said, or something to that effect. Good old college-educated Chico. Harry hoped he was having more luck on his new teaching job than Harry was having on this case.

When Harry got back to the main floor, he noticed two things missing; most of DiGeorgio's sandwich and the collegiate kid.

"What's the matter?" Tanya asked over a new set of music. "You not hungry or something?"

"Hey, your roast beef needs something more than regular booze," Harry said quickly. "You still got some wine downstairs?"

"Yeah, sure, Harry, that's a great idea. I'll get you some."

"Nah," he said lightly. "Stick around. Keep Frank company. That'll be his dessert. I know where the stairs are."

But as soon as Harry left for the kitchen, DiGeorgio lost his appetite. "He's on to something," he said to Tanya.

"Then why didn't he come right out and say so?" she asked.

"Because it could be nothing or it could be nasty," DiGeorgio answered, wiping his mouth with the tablecloth. "Give me a beer and show me the back of this place, will ya?"

The cook responded well when Harry entered.

"Hey, Harry! Long time no see! What is it, you working for the health board now?"

"Take it easy, Mike," Harry replied, walking by quickly. "I, for one, like cat shit."

Mike the cook laughed and turned back to his tureens. Harry continued to a door in the back. Throwing it

43

open and switching on the light, he made his way down the cramped, uneven stairway. One of the three naked bulbs that illuminated the large basement was out, so the far end was in darkness. Harry stopped for as long as it took him to pull out his .44 Magnum. Its barrel gleamed in the cellar's yellow light.

Harry carefully worked his way through the racks of food and beverage. These steel shelves were indiscriminately placed all over the enclosure so he had to move constantly. He took notice of the walls on either side. The building had known many owners so the structure was made of many products. One section was mortared stone, another was crumbling plaster, a third was boarded up. It was like that all over the basement.

He had made it past the canned goods when the whumping started. Harry was taken off guard so he spun to pinpoint the noise's location. Then he realized it was only the muffled bass beat of the disco music upstairs. He turned back toward the far wall and moved deeper into the darkness.

The music and the coolness of the cellar gave Harry's search an eerie edge. He looked in every corner of the cellar, trying to make a connection in his mind. He knew the men's room had windows that opened out on a next door alley, but where did the ladies' room windows open to? If he had it figured right, there had to be a connection in this cellar.

He came up empty. After searching the entire length twice, Harry admitted to himself that he was alone. He was about to attribute the whole thing to frustration over Tucker when he heard bass beats. They were out of sync with the music upstairs.

Harry followed the sounds. They were like uneven pumps of air through a tight valve, making muffled bleats that ended on a slightly higher note. They were coming from the back wall, behind the wine rack.

There was a small hole in the wall. Between the bottles there was a space on the back wall made by some planks and some bricks that didn't quite fit together. Harry leaned down and looked through the hole.

44

He saw short-hair, collegiate, and two other guys raping the second girl.

The light from the ladies' room windows made it clear enough. There was a space between the lavatory and the cellar. And in that space short-hair was holding the auburn-haired girl's head in her lap; one hand clenched in her red hair, the other holding the girl's panties in her mouth. Collegiate was holding down her arms on either side of short-hair's sitting form. Another guy was holding her ankles around the final guy's raping form. They were all positioned in such a way that the raper had his back to Harry. The leg-holder was a bit to Harry's right while the other two were facing him, but too intent on their writhing victim to notice the cop's face in the darkness beyond the little hole in the wall.

Harry put his weapon away. As good as he was, he didn't see a way of nailing all four without hurting the girl. But if he could split them up, he might be able to pick them off. Harry studied the hole. It was about five inches wide and four inches tall, surrounded by crumbling cement and rotting wood. Harry judged the rapist to be about twenty inches away from the hole. Harry took off his jacket.

Harry clenched and unclenched his fists. Harry took two deep, silent breaths. Harry took up a solid position in front of the hole. Harry reached in and wrapped his right arm around the rapist's neck.

"You remember what it was like being born?" he asked.

Then he pulled.

The rapist's head slammed into the wall with the speed and power of a wrecking ball. Harry felt the concrete scrape against the back of his hand, then the material gave way and he was smashing the rapist's shoulders against the widening hole. He wrapped his other hand around the rapist's neck and kept pulling. The wall held for a minute, then opened to let the bastard through.

Harry hauled the choking, terrified rapist through the wall, through the wine bottles, and across the metal rack. Glass and liquid exploded in every direction from the force of Harry's violent maneuver. He pulled until the rapist's head was directly in front of him then swung to the side and threw the guy away.

The rapist flew headfirst into another metal rack, bringing it down with him. He came to a rest, his neck broken, twisted among ten-pound cans of tomatoes.

Harry's Magnum was out before he even let completely go of the rapist. He pointed it through the bigger hole just as short-hair was whipping out a switchblade. She hauled the victim's head back to expose her neck and brought the blade up, snarling.

Harry shot her between the tits.

Even before her back exploded out, the two remaining guys were crawling through the lavatory windows. Harry wasn't going to be particular whether Collegiate bought it next, so he shot through the first window that came into his sights. One of the remaining rapists blew into the ladies' room in a shower of crimson liquid and glittering glass. The last guy slithered all the way through and hauled ass for the ladies' room door.

Harry got a bead on the retreating figure. It was Collegiate. He was squeezing the trigger when the victim's head floated into his view, her eyes tightly closed, tears rolling down her blood-splattered face, her mouth open in a silent wail and short-hair's hand still tightly clenched in her hair. Harry let his trigger finger go slack. He lowered his gun just as the bathroom door slammed shut behind the last rapist.

Collegiate tore down the hall to the men's room, knocking over a coed couple in the process. In mortal fear that the big guy with the big gun might be coming after him, he slammed through the men's room door, roared past the urinals and dove headfirst through the window. He fell into the alleyway headfirst, cutting himself badly on the broken glass.

The panic-stricken kid rolled and crashed up against the alley wall. He looked back through the broken window. The lavatory was empty. The big guy wasn't coming after him that way. Collegiate nearly cried with relief. He was all set to take off into the night when DiGeorgio stuck the barrel of his service revolver against the kid's neck.

"Going somewhere?" he inquired. What DiGeorgio lacked in originality he made up for in timing.

Harry crawled into the newly widened hole between the cellar and the ladies' room wall. He pried short-hair's fingers from the auburn hair. Using a piece of the victim's torn dress, he wiped the blood from the crying girl's face. Then he wrapped his jacket around her waist to cover what had been exposed. Then, gently, he took the auburn-haired girl in his arms. Later, he carried her upstairs.

Her name was Faye, and she didn't like pretty girls. Collegiate told them everything back at headquarters. Faye, it seemed, had a real interesting way of showing her dislike of pretty girls. Faye would make deals. Faye would make deals with guys who liked pretty girls a little too much. Faye would make deals with guys who pretty girls didn't like at all.

The first guy Faye made a deal with wound up being Megan Fullmer's last date. Faye perfected her technique with several deals after that. The date would cover for Faye, and Faye would provide a cover for the date. While it would seem a rapist stole the girl from the date, Faye discovered the best way to get a girl from her date was to have the date be the rapist.

Harry and DiGeorgio were happy to collect all the previous dates that very morning. With Collegiate's confession, it was child's play to knock the others' stories. By midday, the Fullmer case had netted four murderers.

"That's what I love about this job," Harry said with disgust. "It's a showcase for humanity's ingenuity. The fucking ways they think up for killing each other off . . . ."

DiGeorgio snorted and went back to his 1977 *Playboy*. The Playmate of the Month was the one with the blonde hair all the way to her ass. Harry leaned back in his chair and closed his eyes as DiGeorgio turned the magazine sideways and folded out. Harry was thinking about his next move on the Tucker case when Sergeant Reineke walked in.

"I've got good news and bad news, Harry," he said without a smile "The good news is they just found a girl answering McCarthy's description in L.A."

Harry opened his eyes and sat up. "The bad news?"

"She's got a 44 slug in her."

Harry leaned back. Slowly. DiGeorgio put the *Playboy* down on the desk and snorted. "You win some and you lose some." he said.

Harry got up and put on his coat. He stopped beside Reineke on the way out. "Tell Confucius to find another partner," he told the sergeant. "I'll be in L.A."

Candice McCarthy was dead. Harry Callahan was tired. Los Angeles Homicide Detective Lester Shannon was disgusted They all were in the bridal suite of a North Hollywood hotel.

"Unbelievable." Shannon was saying. "He made the reservation by phone, paid a small time stoolie to check in and get the key then carried his 'bride' over the threshold in broad daylight."

Harry didn't look up from the girl's still figure on the blood-soaked bed Her arms were up, tied to the brass headboard Her mouth was open, filled with a terry washcloth held in place with one of her stockings. Her green silk shirt was open exposing the bullet wound in the middle of her chest The coroner had said that her eyes were open under the handkerchief blindfold.

"Anybody see them come in?" Harry asked the muscular L.A. detective.

"Yeah. a lady whose window faced the entrance. She watched them because she thought they looked so cute. The bride had her arms around her hubbie's neck and wore a veil. The groom wore a wide-brimmed hat pulled down low and had a coat draped over his shoulders with the collar up The lady upstairs couldn't see the girl's hands or the guy's face."

"Didn't she think it strange that the girl was wearing a veil with a green shirt and jeans?"

"She wasn't wearing jeans by then," Shannon answered. "She had on a long skirt. And the lady thought the veil was cutest of all. A blow struck for tradition and all that."

Harry nodded and sighed. He noticed a variety of different clothes scattered around the room, including the denims and long skirt. The skirt had covered the ropes around McCarthy's ankles, the veil had covered the gag in her mouth and the coat had covered the bindings on her wrists. The hitman was very professional and very sick. He took a chance by bringing a live witness into a motel to kill her but he must have really got off on it.

"He couldn't leave her alive," Shannon muttered. "What was it?" he asked Harry, "A question of pride?"

"A question of identification," answered Harry. "Anybody else see him?"

"No. He ordered everything through room service, had the waiter leave his meals outside the door and left the signed bill with the leftovers."

"And naturally he left without paying up."

"Naturally," said Shannon, his handsome face screwing into an expression of distaste. "He left her as collateral," he concluded, motioning to the corpse on the bed.

"How about the stoolie who fronted for him at the desk?" Harry inquired further.

"The manager remembers him as a short, wiry guy, like an ex-jockey or something," Shannon described. "We have him figured as Little Brian Heald, a guy who works over at the Warner's lot."

"Pick him up yet?"

"The positive I.D. came through just when you showed up," Shannon blandly replied, watching the rest of his men troop into the room and start wrapping the body up. "I'll do it personally when we're through here."

"We're through here," Harry declared pointedly. "Let's go."

Shannon didn't need much convincing. For a homicide detective, his demeanor was as bland as his face was handsome. Harry pegged him for a failed actor turned cop. Not only did he take directions willingly, he couldn't seem to stay quiet. He always had to keep himself entertained, performing for his audience of one.

Los Angeles was like that all over, Harry decided, looking out the window of Shannon's unmarked car. If you weren't working on a movie, you weren't working. Even Heald, known about town as a small-time hood, did his nine-to-five at a studio. Harry could see Heald practicing his Richard Widmark laugh and Shannon wishing he lived at 77 Sunset Strip.

"Listen," Shannon interrupted his thoughts, "if this hitman was so hot to keep himself a secret, why did he kidnap the girl at all? Why didn't he just kill her at the park along with the Garris kid?"

"I don't know," Harry answered irritably, "Maybe he was homicidal and horny."

Shannon laughed at that. Harry scowled and looked out the window. They were heading for the Warner Studio lot along Barham Boulevard, treating the San Francisco inspector to the sights of wide, nearly empty sidewalks and wide, nearly full open-air restaurants.

"No, really," Shannon pressed. "It's like he doesn't want anyone to know what he looks like, but he wants everyone to know he did it."

"Yeah," Harry replied drily. He stared at the palm trees, stores, and one-story cement, adobe, and paneled dwellings as they seemed to zip by the car. He had to admit to himself that Shannon's question and theory were valid. It would be hard for Harry to believe that the mystery hitman was just a joke-playing, bloodthirsty psycho, although all the signs pointed to it.

But Harry kept looking behind the facts. Why had the guy chopped up two innocent kids at the amusement park? Why drag a girl from Fullerton to L.A. only to kill her in a honeymoon hotel? Why be such a slavering bastard about the whole thing?

He was getting a very uncomfortable feeling about the whole Tucker investigation. The hitman had killed the sheriff in the most spectacular way possible, then he seemed intent on leaving a trail that was about as subtle as a thermonuclear attack. Why, Harry kept asking himself. Why not bury the girl's body so there'd be nothing to bring either the Fullerton or San Fran force to L.A.? And why leave a live stoolie around to put the finger on him? Even if Heald got his orders over the phone, he was still around to say that he did. At the very least, Harry would know he was heading in the right direction.

It didn't make sense. Up until now, no one could get a line on this particular hitman. Unless he had started his business with Tucker, that anonymity was the sign of a pro. So why was a pro leaving a trail of blood crumbs for Harry to follow? The whole thing stunk worse than the drunk tank on Sunday morning.

"Here we are," Shannon announced, turning onto the Warner lot. Harry looked up while the L.A. detective flashed his I.D. to the gate guard. Directly in front of them was an old fashioned water tower marked "The Burbank Studios." All around that were two- and three-story buildings, nestled amidst trees, hills and greenery. Shannon didn't ask for any information or directions. The L.A. detective knew where he was going. Harry figured he had been to the studio as many times before as he could manage Shannon just silently drove along a multicolored line painted on the dark pavement.

"Those color lines direct visitors to different departments," he explained to Harry. "Heald works in the delivery department, which crosses the blue line."

"Uh-huh," Harry answered, seeing a speed bump up ahead.

As soon as Shannon had slowed to cross the mound, Harry opened his door and hopped out. Shannon braked in surprise. Before the L.A. cop could say anything, however, Harry had laid his hands on the open passenger's window and leaned down to elaborate.

"There's no way Heald could think he wouldn't be recognized. If he's here at all, he'll be waiting for us. Just in case he wants to do it the hard way, I'll be waiting for him around back."

Shannon, true to Harry's estimation of him, nodded and drove on. After the cop car had turned out of sight, Harry had to admit to himself that he'd rather work with bland Shannon than Sergeant Baker of Fullerton. But

51

whether Shannon had the sense of DiGeorgio was yet to be determined. Harry started walking along the blue line.

About fifty feet around the next corner, Harry passed a sign pointing out the messenger office as being only a trailer on the other side of the back lot. Harry left the blue line and started across a parking lot located in between a row of dressing rooms and a three-story office building.

Just as he was moving around the right side of the latter structure, dozens of men dressed in cowboy outfits emerged from the former locale, shepherded by a small, bespectacled, mustached man with a megaphone and a clipboard.

"Don't walk on the grass, OK?" the man called through the amplifier. "OK, guys, you know your places from yesterday, right? They're all ready on location with the same scene as yesterday, all right? Just a little more energy and a little more action and we can get it in the can today. All right, OK?"

The extras didn't deem to answer. They just trooped toward Harry, walking on anything they wanted. Harry slowed his pace so that he blended in with the buckskin. It was a good camouflage. Heald wouldn't spot him even if he were looking at this crowd.

"Hey, you!" Harry heard the megaphone man call. "Hey! Why aren't you in costume? Hey, the guy in brown. The tall guy. Hey!"

It wasn't until the third "hey" that Harry realized the man was talking to him. Not wanting to leave the cover of the crowd, he simply raised his hand in an "A-OK" sign, hoping the man would take for granted that Harry knew what he was doing. But he had underestimated the superiority complexes of assistant directors. He had just made it to the edge of the Western set when the megaphone man caught up with him.

"Listen, Stilt," the short, intense man said, "I'm talking to you. Where's your costume?"

Without slowing his stride, Harry answered. "You're only the second person who's ever called me 'Stilt.' I didn't slug the first one because he was carrying a gun. You're only carrying a megaphone."

The man slowed and put his hands up in supplication. "I'm only asking a question, for Chrissake," he said to no one in particular. "I'm only doing my job. Hey, are you on the list?" he called after Harry, flipping through the pages on his clipboard. "Hey, what's your number?"

Not having a number and not being on the list, Harry took the moment to break off from the sea of extras, moving into an alley between two Western mockups. Trotting down the worn path, he noticed that only the front of the buildings were wild Western. They were just facades stuck onto what looked like inner-city brownstones.

Harry reached the rear of the set and spotted the messenger trailer across the way. There were only a group of trees, a small forest, separating him from his quarry. As he watched, Shannon's car pulled into the trailer parking area. Harry looked back toward the Western street. The megaphone man was framed in the alley opening, still checking his list and scanning the crowd of cowboys. Harry smiled, turned back toward the trailer, and set off for the woods.

Just as he reached the first tree, a tiny, thin man burst out the rear door of the trailer, a veritable tornado of swirling papers in his wake. Harry remained motionless until the harried figure of Lester Shannon appeared in the back door opening, his hair disheveled, his face red, and his feet kicking at a few boxes in his way.

"Goddamn it, Heald!" the L.A. detective shouted. "Halt, would ya?"

The stoolie didn't look like he intended to even slow down. The little guy was tearing up the dirt toward the back lot. Harry momentarily considered bringing him down with a Magnum bullet, but after a second's thought, left his weapon where it was. A damaged Heald wouldn't help at all come interrogation time. Instead, Harry ambled back the way he had come.

The stoolie and the San Francisco cop both arrived on the Western set at the same time. It was the time when the director called "action!"

In order to save time, the crew was shooting simul-

53

taneously inside the bar and out on the street. Inside the bar, stuntmen dressed as cowboys were struggling on a two-story interior set. Outside, more men were fake fighting on the bar's balcony and on the street proper. Crawling around the floor, seated behind the bar, and set up behind the camera were special-effects people, ready to detonate various blood bags, exploding glass, and bullet holes on cue.

Not one of them noticed as Heald raced into the bar through the back way with Harry close behind.

The scene was well choreographed. The bar was packed wall to wall with swinging men. They were swinging their fists, swinging their bodies over bannisters, into chairs, onto tables, and down stairs. One man was even swinging from the chandelier.

Little Brian Heald burst into the scene from the rear, bumping into a stuntman. That stuntman was about to dodge a roundhouse right. Heald knocked him right into the swing.

Both actors were rocked by the connection. Heald slipped by just as the man on the receiving end flew back into Harry Callahan's arms. Quickly recovering, the punched man found his feet, whirled around, and slugged the cop in the jaw.

Harry's head snapped back, but the rest of his body remained motionless. He heard his brain hum and his eyes clouded, but only for a second. Blinking his momentarily misty eyes, Harry looked at the stuntman. He could see real anger in the fighting man's face, so he straight-armed the actor in the neck.

The stuntman choked, stumbled back a step, then fell to his knees. Directly behind him another actor was supposed to run toward the stairs. Instead he fell over the choking man. The man behind him was supposed to fake a punch toward another directly in front of him. But because of the falling man's kicking feet pushing him forward, the punch became real. The man's fist just glanced off the target's shoulder, but it was enough to throw his practiced response off. Instead of falling across the bar itself, the stuntman collided into two other fighters.

54

Heald saw which way the fake fight was going. He took advantage of the situation by pushing as many stuntmen as he could into each other and slithering away just as Harry got close to him. Invariably the enraged stuntmen would whirl to see who pushed them and invariably Harry would be standing there.

The first attacker tried to knee Callahan in the balls. Harry threw the bottom of his body back and threw the flat of his hand into the man's nose. The first attacker fell backward, a column of blood marking his fall.

The second attacker complicated matters by taking a swing at Harry while an off-set technician set off a "squib" on the man's chest by remote control. Callahan ducked under the swing just as the small explosive attached to a steel plate on the man's chest blew out, ripping open a fake blood bag. The stuntman's fist missed the cop, but the crimson gore caught Harry full in the face.

The cop straightened with his face dripping red. Harry put both hands on the second attackers shoulder and pushed. Off balance because of his missed punch, the stuntman fell on his side.

The third and fourth attackers came from two sides. The third was another Heald-primed stuntman. The fourth was a guy who had witnessed Harry's retaliation against the first and second. The third swung his right arm back, trying to hit whoever pushed him without turning around. The fourth hopped over the downed second man, his fists clenched for the kill.

Harry reached in between the clenched fists to grab the latter attacker by the shirt front. With an abrupt jerk, he pulled the fourth guy's head into the third's backward trajectory. One man's knuckles collided with the other's lips. Harry dropped the latter and sidestepped the former just in time to see Heald crawling toward the front door. Unfortunately, there were still about a dozen guys between him and the stoolie.

With an angry shout, Harry started hauling actors out of his way. When the third cameraman suddenly saw a bloody man in modern dress plowing through its line of sight, it reported it by radio to the assistant director.

After the assistant told the director, an abrupt halt was called to the proceedings. But no matter how many "cuts" were called, the stuntmen were too far gone to stop. By that time the fight was real for them.

Even Heald was getting caught up in the brawl. When he saw Harry barreling toward him, he scrambled to his feet and pulled a six gun out of a struggling stuntman's holster. Still backing toward the door, he opened up on the rampaging Harry. The stoolie was wondering why the "bullets" weren't having any effect when two more stuntmen ran in to join the fray. They smacked right into Heald, sending the blank-filled gun spinning to the floor and the stoolie spinning under a table.

At that juncture, the assistant director came roaring in, screaming at the top of his lungs.

"Cut! Cut, goddamn it! Didn't you hear the director? Cut, for Chrissake!"

Finally the huge bunch of stuntmen started to respond, but there were still too many milling and rolling about for Harry to get to Heald. The assistant director was having no trouble getting to Harry, however. He plowed straight through until he was screaming up into Callahan's still-wet face.

"I told you to get a costume, Stilt! What the hell are you trying to do? Do you know how much money you've cost this production? It's coming out of your pay, you hear me, Stilt? You're getting no money, all right? What's your number, Stilt? What's your fucking number?" The man pulled up his clipboard for a renewed search for Harry's name.

Harry looked at Heald. The stoolie was sneaking out from under the table. With a few steps he'd be out. Harry looked at the man rifling through his clipboard. Then he put his left hand around the assistant director's neck and his right hand around the man's belt.

With a mighty tug and a subsequent swing, Harry threw the assistant director across the room and onto the tabletop. The man with the clipboard landed back first, scattering the drinks, cards, and poker chip props. The table's legs collapsed, leaving the full weight of the surprised man and wooden circle on Little Brian Heald.

Harry took his time making his way across the room. Then he casually reached down and pulled Heald to his feet. Holding the stoolie tightly by the collar, Harry stared down at the dazed assistant director.

"I told you about the 'Stilt' thing before," he said.

"I didn't do anything, I don't know anything, I don't understand what yer askin' me!" Little Brian Heald plaintively asserted.

"Oh, you did something all right," Lester Shannon retorted, leaning against the back of the chair the stoolie was sitting on. "You picked up the key and signed your own name for a bridal suite."

"Yeah? So? I needed someplace to stay."

"You didn't stay there, Brian, me boy," Shannon retorted.

"Sure. Sure I did. It was my name on the register, right?"

"So you killed Candice McCarthy," Harry Callahan said quietly, sitting opposite his captured quarry.

Little Brian swallowed. "What?" he choked. "What?"

"Candy McCarthy," Shannon repeated, leaning over Heald's head, a broad smile on his handsome face. "A pretty girl. Young. Blond. Had a hole in her chest about this big." He made a circle with his left thumb and forefinger. Heald turned a shallow green.

"Hey, I don't know nothin' about that!" he yelled, getting up.

"Sure you do," Shannon answered easily, pushing him down into his seat again. "You know who paid you to get the key and sign your name, don't you Brian boy?"

"I swear I don't," Heald babbled. "On me mother's grave! He called me. He called me on the phone. He made me leave the key in me mailbox. He told me to go to work. When—when I got home the key was gone and the money was there. I swear!"

"You do a lot of swearing," Shannon said, circling back to where Harry was sitting. "Give me reason to believe you."

Heald poured the whole story out of his brain. He had gotten a call at his home one night. For a goodly sum, he was to reserve, sign, and collect the key from the hotel the next morning. He was to leave the key in his own mailbox. He was to spend the money. He was to ask no questions. He didn't think of any to ask until Shannon came looking for him. He ran because he was a natural runner. It was an instinct the Healds had held in good stead for many, many years.

"That's all he said?" Harry slowly inqured.

"Yeah . . . yeah. That's all."

Shannon shook his head just as slowly. "Bri, Bri, Bri. You still haven't said anything worth saying. My sense of disbelief is still intact. Think harder."

"Good God, Shannon, you can't do this to me! I'm one of yer own brother Irishmen . . .

"Yer no brother o'mine," Shannon spat with an exaggerated accent. "*I* said think harder. Is that all *he* said?"

"Mother of God, Shannon, I swear . . . wait a minute. Wait just a mintue . . . ."

Outwardly, the cops' expressions didn't change. Shannon still leaned on the back of Harry's chair. He stared at the fingers of his right hand. Callahan grew very still. If the room got any quieter, they might have heard his insides boiling.

"That's right," Heald continued, a smile of relief breaking across his face, "I was impressed with what he was paying. I remember now. I asked him if he wanted anything else done while he was in town. He said, 'No, I've got to get back to John Wayne's graveyard.' That's what he said. 'I've got to get back to John Wayne's graveyard.' "

Shannon kept staring at his fingernails. Harry didn't move.

"That's it!" Heald cried in desperation. "I swear!"

"Man," Shannon finally said. "You talk about your disappointments. I haven't felt this letdown since I went to *The Shining*. With all your drunken imagination, you can't come up with anything better than that?"

"On me mother's grave, Shannon, it's the truth!" Heald nearly screamed. "You can't pin this killin' on me! You can't!"

Shannon held up a finger and smiled, his perfect, white teeth grinding against each other. "Watch," he said. He lowered his finger onto the intercom button resting on the interrogation room table. "Sergeant, you can collect the suspect now."

Heald was yelling all the way out into the hall and down to the detention cells. After the stoolie was dragged out, Shannon sat down in the vacated chair.

"Cops come and cops go," he sighed, "but one thing that never changes is our sadistic sense of humor."

"Could you pin this on him?" Harry asked.

"In this fucked-up town, anything is possible," Shannon answered. "What do you think?"

"I think he's good at what he does."

Shannon snorted.

"There's no way a pro is going to hire a renowned stoolie unless he wants something spilled," Harry continued with disgust. "And there's no way you can forget a line like 'John Wayne's graveyard.'"

Shannon clasped his hands on the table and leaned in. "What the hell is going on, Callahan? What the hell have you gotten me into?"

The San Francisco cop's mind clamped onto the truth like a vise chomping onto a gun barrel. This guy was a pro. But he was a pro with a purpose. He had been leaving dead bodies around like letters of a marquee. He wanted attention for a particular reason. And the reason was enough to make Harry's mouth fill with the flavor of ash.

"Its' not your problem anymore," he told Shannon.

"Come on, you heard Heald's brilliantly executed declaration. John Wayne's graveyard is right here. Every cop in California will be after this guy."

"He's not in California anymore," Harry said with certainty.

"What makes you say that?"

"You're the Hollywood detective," Callahan sighed. "You ought to know." Shannon shrugged. Harry lectured. "John Wayne only died in a few of his films . . . ."

"He died in his last one, *The Shootist*, and he died in that war one," Shannon remembered, trying to make up for whatever Harry thought he should have known.

"And he died in *The Alamo*," Harry said, aware of how outlandish it was all getting.

"He directed that one," Shannon related, proud and defensive of his film knowledge. "That and *The Green Berets*."

"Oh, yeah?" said Harry, feigning interest. "Really? Well, the Alamo is in San Antonio . . . the same place Boris Tucker came from."

Lester Shannon suddenly became subdued. He looked at the interrogation tabletop with his lips pursed. Then he smacked his lips, shook his head, and leaned back expansively.

"Man, it's crazy," he said. "What's he doing it all for?"

"Advertising," Harry mumbled.

"What?"

"I said he's advertising."

"What for?" Shannon wanted to know.

"For me," Harry said.

Four

A lot of Southerners talk about San Antonio, but Harry Callahan thought Davy Crockett put it best. "You kin all go to hell, I'm a-goin' to Texas."

The way the modern-day inspector was feeling, those sentiments could be the other way around. Nicely put, his reception back at San Francisco headquarters was not enthusiastic. Trying to explain the hitman's rationale to Lieutenant Bressler was like explaining calculus to a coal miner.

But Harry remained decisive. In order for the assassin to kill Tucker, he had to follow the sheriff from San Antonio to Fullerton. Once arriving in California, the hitman must have known that Tucker arranged a dinner with Harry the day of his death. And once Tucker and Garris were dead, he must've discovered Garris' date was from San Francisco.

It all added up to one thing; the hitman wanted Harry to come after him. Killing a friend, kidnapping a residential girl, leaving behind a stoolie-related clue, it was all part of his warped way to offend Callahan's sensibilities. That sort of personalized logic fell on deaf ears. Neither Bressler nor his superiors could be convinced that Harry had a case.

Instead, Bressler was convinced Harry was working too hard, that he was having paranoid delusions. He suggested Harry take a little time off. Harry agreed. On his own time and with his own money, the cop reserved a ticket to San Antonio, Texas.

Harry's reception in the large Texas city was as chilly as it had been in California. No sooner had he stepped off the plane at the San Antonio International Airport than he found four lawmen waiting for him.

Two of the uniformed men carefully took Harry's bag and suit carrier out of his hands. The third stood by, his hand gently, but noticeably, resting on his holstered gun butt. The fourth, and eldest, officer, dressed in a sheriff's finery, stood directly in front of Harry with a big smile on his face and both thumbs hooked into a thick, wide, gun belt.

As Harry looked slowly and silently at the two standing men and the two others who were diligently tearing his luggage apart, all the other tourists walked around the scene, their happy entry into the town turning into a hushed, hurried exit. The officers of the law hadn't even waited until Callahan got out of the arrival area.

Finally the suitcase search was over. Harry's clothes were strewn across the lounge rug. So far not one word had been spoken. The smug sheriff with the hooked thumbs was the first to break the silence.

"Welcome to San Antonio," he began, his voice a classic Texas twang. "I hope you don't mind but we have reason to suspect a thorough search of yer person might be in orda."

Harry answered by narrowing his eyes, letting his lip infinitesimally curl off his teeth, then raised his arms. The two suitcase searchers approached and patted him down just as casually and callously as they had strewn his luggage about.

Soon his pocket money, key chain, and wallet had joined his clothes on the floor. His belt was taken off, his shoes were removed, and even his cufflinks were scrutinized. Finally the pair of officers moved back, looking at their superior with resignation.

The sheriff moved forward until the top of his cowboy hat was level with Harry's forehead. Pulling out his own long barrel revolver he gently tapped Harry's crotch as he spoke.

"We was jes kinda wonderin', you know, whether you thought about bringin' yer weapon along."

Harry looked down with a slight look of surprise, but when he replied, his voice was a quiet, threatening snarl. "You and I both know that would be illegal."

"That it would," said the sheriff, stopping his tapping. "That it would. Just how long are you fixin' on staying in our fair city, Inspector Callahan?"

"Just long enough to straighten out a few things," said Harry, looking pointedly at the three other cops. Back to the sheriff, he added "not too long at all."

The sheriff's smile wavered a bit, but held on. "Now that's good to hear," he answered pleasantly, motioning to his men to leave. "Y'all take care, hear?" he said to Harry as he backed out of the waiting room.

"You, too," said Harry quietly. Callahan wasn't sure if the sheriff heard him and the sheriff wasn't sure Harry actually said it. Whatever the reason, the Texas lawmen left without further incident.

It was not a good sign, Harry sardonically decided as he surveyed his strewn belongings. Even though his visit was officially described as unofficial, and Lieutenant Bressler certainly wouldn't call ahead to tell the Texas law of his inspector's arrival, the newly replaced sheriff of San Antonio proper knew Harry was coming. He knew far enough ahead to be waiting for him. Harry wondered if the sheriff was the only one who knew.

He discovered the answer soon enough. As the supposedly vacationing Californian did his best to collect his clothes without looking ridiculous, a small group of teenagers collected at the door of the arrival lounge. Harry kept collecting until he noticed that the kids all looked pretty smug and all seemed to know each other.

"Anything I can help you with?" he asked, bent at the waist to retrieve a wrinkled shirt.

"Hey, no, man," said a lanky, angular kid in front wearing a T-shirt, ten-gallon hat, and a tattoo of a bull on his upper arm inscribed with the word "beef." "Can't a guy watch?" he continued.

"It's a free country," said Harry, picking up the shirt, rolling it into a ball and throwing it at his open suitcase.

"Hey, guys, is this what we call Texas hospitality?" said another kid in the back of the group. He was wearing a short-sleeved military-cut shirt and chinos. "Why don't we help the dude?"

"Yeah," said the kid with the tattoo, like it was some kind of brilliant idea. "Want some help, mister?"

"Don't tire yourself," Harry answered offhandedly, scooping up his wallet.

"No, it's OK," said tattoo, leading the rest of the gang into the waiting room, "we can handle it."

The group began to spread out to all four corners of the enclosure. Without making it obvious, Harry counted eight guys altogether.

"Yeah," said a Mexican kid in a rose-colored tank top, "I can get your pants." Harry leaned over to pick up a pair that rested on a plastic chair. The Mexican sat heavily on them. Harry let go, straightened, and turned toward tattoo.

The lead kid was smiling much in the same way the sheriff had been smiling previously. Another kid standing to the left scooped up a pair of cotton briefs. "Yeah, and I can get your shorts."

Harry stood rooted to the spot, not taking his eyes off tattoo. Tattoo just kept smiling.

All around them, the gang started collecting Harry's clothes in earnest. Some threw them around, others ripped them up, the Mexican pulled out a switchblade and cut neat lines in the pant legs, and the kid to the left stuffed the underwear down his own pant front.

Harry continued to stare at the tattooed kid. The longer he stared, the less sure tattoo's smile became. Finally, the kid felt forced to speak.

"Hey, don't even think about slugging me, man,

64

because if you do, you'll spend your vacation in jail."
Tattoo's declaration was higher pitched than his earlier
conversation, and he hit the word "vacation" a little too
hard. To make up for his *faux pas* he continued in a
forcibly lower voice. "And don't go looking for a cop. By
the time you find one, we'll be long gone." Tattoo hit the
"you" hard in that sentence.

Harry just stared.

"OK, guys, let's go," Tattoo hastily ordered, waving
his arm, but keeping one eye on Harry. When Harry
didn't move, even after everybody but Tattoo left, the kid
felt inclined to give the cop some unasked-for advice.

"Hey, man, you're crazy. If I were you, I'd get right
back on that plane and go back where you came from."

"Harry didn't move, but he said, "Thanks."

The kid's eyes widened, he shook his head quickly,
then disappeared from the waiting room door. Harry
waited a few seconds, collected his key chain and cash,
and left the rest for the airport custodians.

While walking down the shiny hallways of the airport toward the taxi stand, Harry whistled "Deep in the
Heart of Texas" and flipped his key chain over and over
in the air. When he wasn't whistling, he was grinning.
Grinning like a wolf who smelled dinner. In spite of his
welcoming committee's lack of warmth, Harry felt good.
He now knew he was in the right place.

He walked up to the first redcap, tapped him on the
shoulder, pointed back to the arrival room, and started
giving instructions. He was halfway through the part
about getting the suitcase repaired when he noticed the
redcap wasn't listening. The redcap was not only disinterested, but he was making a point of being disinterested.
He was looking at the ceiling and leaning on his cart as if
Harry wasn't there.

"Hey, I'm talking to you," said Harry.

The redcap took that as a cue to walk away, pulling
his cart with him. Harry looked to the next redcap in
sight. As soon as that one saw Harry looking at him, he
suddenly became very busy helping an old lady who
looked lost. A third redcap suddenly decided to see what

65

it was like on the other side of the airport. After that, Callahan decided to chuck his luggage along with the clothes and head into town.

He walked outside to the waiting cabs and hopped into the back seat of the first one. If he were lucky, he figured, it would be the hitman himself disguised as the driver, waiting to kill him. No such luck. The driver merely said "on call" without turning around. Harry got out and looked at the taxi sign on the car's roof. It was turned off. He pivoted around to look at the next car in line. As he turned the taxi's off-duty sign went on.

Deciding to be a glutton for punishment, Harry checked all six cabs in line. The next to last three were all using variations on the first two cabbies' excuses. The last cabbie had an original flair. He was out to lunch.

Harry wasn't worried. He wasn't even a little bit pissed. But he did readjust his thinking. All along he had figured that it was some sort of political ramification that got Tucker offed. Callahan couldn't see the late sheriff getting killed by a jealous husband or vengeful crook. For a sheriff to get croaked in as spectacular a fashion as Tucker did means that the man must have tread on some very tender toes. And the tenderest toes Harry knew belonged to politicians.

They may have thick skins and fast minds, but they don't like being crossed. And Tucker was in a position to do a lot of crossing. So Harry had figured that a powerful politico was behind it all along. Now, however, Harry had to amend his reasoning. Anyone powerful enough to mobilize the police, the street gangs, the redcaps, *and* the cabbies went beyond area politics. Harry admitted to himself that he was dealing with a power beyond that. A power of money. A power of business.

In San Antonio, power, money, and business meant one of two things: fuel or food. Here, you made your fortune from either black gold or Black Angus. Houston or Dallas were really the major oil centers, so Harry figured that he might be dealing with a cattleman. Or a farmer. Either way, it was probably a self-made man who was used to destroying things with his own two hands.

And Harry was fixing to face him without jurisdiction, without his Magnum, and without a change of clothes.

"Hey buddy, need a ride?"

Harry turned toward the voice. It had come from the other side of the first taxi. The San Francisco cop squinted over the cab's roof to see a San Antonio cop standing half-in and half-out of his patrol car. Callahan took his time pulling out sunglasses and slipping them on. In the reduced glare he noted the car was devoid of markings like "Property of the Sheriff's Office." It was a good old regular San Antonio police car.

The driver probably wasn't a good old regular San Antonio police officer, however. No cop in any state was known for offering rides to tall, craggy strangers in airports. Harry's mind harkened back to the "Vigilante Cop" case for a second, then eliminated the connection from his mind. It was unlikely a uniformed cop could kill a visiting plainclothesman in a cop car without raising interdepartmental ire.

Naw, it wouldn't be worth it, Harry thought, and he did have to get into town somehow. He took a moment to look around. Too hot to walk, he decided, then moved over to the passenger side of the patrol vehicle.

"Heading for the Ramada Inn?" Harry inquired.

"I can handle it," replied the uniformed patrolman, getting in. Harry followed his lead and hopped in the back. The first thing he noticed was the back of another cop's head. The bright Texas sun was reflecting off the windshield, so even with his sunglasses Harry didn't spot the driver's partner. The second thing he noticed was that there was no grating between the front and rear seats. Usually they had a cage arrangement separating the arresting officer in the front seat from the "alleged perpetrator" in the back.

If Harry had spent less time checking out the inadequacies of the patrol car and more time double-checking his environment, he might have seen something interesting. He might have seen the first cab driver pick up his pad and write down the number of the cop car. He might have seen the cabbie's wide face stare out the window after him. He might have seen the man's thin lips spread into a tight smile. He might have seen the acne scars on both cheeks. He might have seen the face of the man in the white overalls.

The San Francisco homicide inspector had been half-right and almost lucky. The hitman was disguised and was waiting to kill him, but not at that time and place. The assassin was doing what all good assassins do; watching the victim react. He wanted to be ready when the time came to eliminate Dirty Harry Callahan.

His employer had arranged the whole airport stonewall, but he saw no reason why he shouldn't take the opportunity to examine his future target. He also saw no reason to inform his employer. He had his own connections. They had gotten him the cab. Minutes after throwing Harry out of the taxi, in fact, the hitman took a family of four to the Air Force Village on the other side of town.

Instead of taking Route 410 to the military center of San Antonio, the patrol car went straight down San Pedro Avenue, through Almos Park, to the center of town. Instead of noticing the seven hundred fifty-foot Tower of the Americas or the Freeman Coliseum, Harry kept picking up more and more idiosyncrasies about the patrol car. Harry hadn't ridden in a San Francisco model for years and had never seen the San Antonio version, but all the outfitting here told him this particular car was ancient.

"So you're Harry Callahan," said the driver out of the blue.

"Everybody else knows it," Harry retorted. "Why not you."

The driver laughed honestly and openly. It wasn't the laugh of a man eager for a confrontation. "Yeah, well, Hannibal Striker isn't exactly a charter member of the Welcome Wagon. You're lucky he didn't send you packing back to San Francisco."

"Yeah, instead he destroys my packing. Who the hell is Hannibal Striker?"

"Calls himself H. A. Striker," the partner suddenly said without turning around. "His real name Edd Villaveda; a wetback made good. He called himself Hannibal until 'Dallas' became such a big hit, then he changed it to H. A. He thinks it makes him closer to J. R., the villain on that show. He likes people to associate his name with power and wealth.

"He likes gaining power and wealth. He likes using power and wealth. In San Antonio, he is power and wealth."

Harry leaned up to get a glimpse of the cops in the front seat. "OK, now I know who Striker is, and you know who I am. Would you mind telling me who the hell are you?"

The partner turned to face Harry. He was a nice, innocent-looking guy with a sharp nose, cleft chin, and hollow cheeks. "I'm Peter C. Nash," he said, tipping his police cap. "And this is a friend of mine," he concluded, pointing the back of the cap at the driver. When he pulled off the hat, he exposed a nearly bald head, encircled on three sides by a band of nearly white hair.

"Nash," Callahan repeated, ". . . you're the one Dotty Tucker mentioned."

"Yes," Nash replied quietly. "I was Sheriff Tucker's deputy."

"Dotty also thought you were the one who got Tucker killed," Harry revealed calmly.

Nash pondered Callahan's words for a few moments before answering. "She's probably right," he said sadly. "Tucker was a good sheriff who was made into a great one. Great law officers don't last very long around Striker. When Tucker couldn't be bought, couldn't be framed, and couldn't be voted out of office, there was only one way left to get rid of him. He was killed for doing his job too well."

It was a new twist, thought Harry. Usually a seemingly impeachable lawman was exposed to be inept, corrupt, and vicious upon examination. Tucker, it seems, was too good for his own good. "And where do you fit in, Nash?" he asked aloud.

"I arranged for him to do his job too well," the man said earnestly. "I arranged all the busts and had Tucker move in for the actual kill."

"So he got all the credit and became the main target."

"Yeah," said Nash with what sounded like honest regret. "I wasn't interested in the 'dirty' side of the job. Tucker kept telling me it had to be done, so I let him do it."

"That's funny," said Harry. "Usually the research, the stake-outs, and the setups are considered the dirty work."

"Not to me," Nash said with enthusiasm. "With the proper amount of background work, I created arrests that were seamless. We had the best prosecution ratio in the Midwest. Ask the D.A. Ask any D.A.!"

"So now you've been busted back to the beat," Harry assumed, waving a hand at the out-of-date car interior.

"No, sir," said Nash. "I quit as soon as the word of Tucker's killing came in."

"So what do you call this patrol car, then?" Harry wanted to know. "Where did you get those uniforms?"

"You can't spend a couple of years on the San Antonio police force without making some connections," said Nash with a smile. "There are still a few good cops left. All this was supplied to us."

"What for? Why the charade?"

"Protection," said Nash. "I said there were still a few good cops left, but there are still a lot of cops on Striker's payroll. Like the new sheriff who met you at the airport."

Callahan remembered the smug ball-buster and his trio of goons. He began to realize what Nash was up against. "That was Tucker's replacement?"

"Grown, nurtured, and groomed by Striker," Nash acknowledged, "and then H. A. used his influence to get him into office."

"The right honorable Sheriff Mitch Strughold," the driver drawled sarcastically.

"Once he got in," Nash continued, "he brought a whole mess of strong-arms with him. The whole office is under Striker's thumb now."

"That still doesn't answer my question," Harry contended. "What's with the dress-up and dance number you're pulling?"

70

Nash looked at the driver then stole an incongruous glance out the side window as if he were afraid passing bugs were outfitted with electronic bugs.

"There's a war going on in this town," he told Harry in the hushed tones of a back-room conspirator. "And a war doesn't stop because the General has been killed. I'm still working on destroying all of Striker's dirty deals. I get as much help as my allies are able to give me. But we need a new general.

"I can get an out-of-use patrol car to confuse anyone watching. As far as Striker's informers are concerned you were picked up by a non-existent pair of officers. What I can't get is someone to do the dirty work Tucker used to do. All the guys have wives and families and they really need their jobs."

"I'd be up shit's creek if Strughold knew I even did this," the driver interceded.

"So what you want is a hired gun," concluded Callahan.

"In a way," conceded Nash.

"If Striker can do it, why can't we?" the driver demanded with emotion.

Harry lowered his head, smiling in amazement. San Francisco could get pretty weird at times and he would be the last one to say interpolice relationships were always tops, but at least he didn't have two separate cop armies battling each other.

"Well, you're out of luck with me," he finally said. "I don't even have a gun."

In response, Nash leaned down to the floor of the front seat and came up with a sleek, well-stained walnut box. He handed it to Harry. The inspector recognized it immediately. It was a brand-spanking-new gun case, large enough to house a high-powered handgun. Harry lifted the top.

Sure enough, resting in a sea of green cloth was a shining bright blue Magnum .44 revolver with a six and a half inch barrel.

"I told you I had connections," Nash said proudly.

Harry hefted the weapon. It had the weight and feel of his own. It was a Smith and Wesson Model 29 with a

71

checked hammer, a grooved trigger, a front Red Ramp sight, and a rear Micrometer Click sight which was adjustable for elevation and windage. It was a beautiful weapon, which Harry knew how to use. Once some people knew how to ride a bike, they could ride any make or model. So it was with Harry and his handgun.

But the Magnum was not the most impressive thing in the box. The most impressive thing was the license underneath. The paper, duly signed and witnessed by Tucker and Nash, allowed Harry to carry the weapon on his person anywhere within the city borders.

"This still legal?" Harry asked Nash.

"Check the date," the ex-deputy answered.

Sure enough, the document was good for an entire year. Callahan laid the gun and the license back onto the soft material, closed the box, and minutely shook his head with regret.

"What you want me to be is an enforcer," he said thoughtfully. "I was an enforcer once and I lost something close to me."

"Yeah, that terrorist thing," Nash commiserated. "We know all about it."

"That's another thing," Harry noted. "Everybody seems to know everything about me. Striker knew I was coming, you knew I was coming, and you're all waiting and watching for my next move. The stakes are high and the odds are near impossible. Give me one good reason I should take the place of Tucker."

"Sweetboy Williams," Nash said immediately.

"What?"

"Sweetboy Williams," Nash repeated. "H. A. Striker's hired gun. He thinks he's the last of the great gunfighters. He's a gung-ho cowboy, a real John Wayne freak, and Striker's favorite hitman. He's the man most likely to have shot the sheriff."

Harry became pensive. "He use a .44?"

"Yeah."

"A John Wayne freak?"

"Knows all his movies backward and forward and thinks he's living one."

Harry sighed, leaned back, and closed his eyes. The trio drove in silence for a while. The cop car driver tooled past the Alamo Stadium, Brackenridge Park, and almost reached Fort Sam Houston before Harry spoke again.

"Anybody know where I can get a second pair of pants cheap?" he asked. "It looks like I'll be staying in town a while."

"I want him," said Sweetboy Williams.

"You can't have him," said Hannibal Striker, fingering a tomato. When it didn't suit his tender appraisal, the man once known as Edd Villaveda hurled the red globe into the four-foot-high fireplace behind him. "Be reasonable," the Mexican-American businessman implored his muscular lunch guest. "Here is a San Francisco inspector on an ostensive vacation. It wouldn't be as easy to convince out-of-state authorities he blew his brains out."

"No problem," the hitman replied reasonably, his voice loaded with mock surprise. "A depressed lawman, despondent over a friend's death, his own life rife with tragedy, decides to kill himself in sunny San Antonio. And the bullet would be from a .44 Magnum. What could be simpler?"

"And what would be stupider?" Striker replied sharply, pushing the plate of vegetables away from him. "Remember, I have no authority in California. The only reason the Tucker thing worked is that there was no one here interested in pursuing the matter. If Inspector Callahan were to die under suspicious circumstances, there'd be no way I could prevent a full-scale, indepth San Francisco investigation."

Sweetboy Williams rose abruptly from the large, circular table and moved over to the sumptious walls of the dining room. Fingering the intricate inlaid wooden carvings and staring at the various ancient weapons displayed at set intervals, he defended himself.

"The only reason the Tucker thing worked is that I made it work," he declared. "I can make Callahan's death work."

"No matter how innocent his death looked," Striker

soothed the assassin, "it would still raise questions back in his department. We mustn't let him die on Texan soil. I say watch and wait."

"And I say he must die now," Sweetboy stressed. "Before it's too late. He could destroy everything you've built."

"You give him too much credit," the businessman said quietly, iron-hard assurance in his voice. "No one man can disturb my system."

"Tucker did," Sweetboy reminded him.

"And now Tucker is gone," Striker reminded him back.

"I killed him," the hitman retorted.

"On my instructions," the businessman concluded, rising from the table. He placed both sets of knuckles on the pristeen white tablecloth and leaned over the basket of multicolored flowers in the linen's center. "This is the last time I shall remind you. You work for me. You follow my instructions. You have entered my home and my confidence by being the best at what you do. What you do is enforce my wishes. I instruct, you accomplish. I visualize, you realize. Is that clear?"

"Clear," Sweetboy said simply and immediately. He would get nowhere if he started balking against the wetback now.

"Good," said Striker casually, resuming his seat. "Come have some dessert. I'm sure it will make up for what the meal lacked." He rang for service as the hitman returned to the table.

Sweetboy could be slick when he wanted to be. That was part and parcel of his charm. Ever since his hooker mother had named him Sweetboy because of his angelic face and happy demeanor, he saw himself as being the most affable of survivors. Through the ravages of childhood and life with a prostitute, Sweetboy had kept his humor by becoming sardonic and by escaping into Western fantasies.

His style was as natural as Striker's style was extrinsic. The businessman had found it necessary to change his name when he entered into a partnership with an Anglo vegetable merchant. From those formative years he retained a vegetarian's appetite and a deep-seated hate of Anglos. He stayed in the partnership until he knew enough to force the white half out and take over. Following that came years of expansion and education. Edd Villaveda wanted it all and thought it necessary to change his personality in order to get it.

He started with his name, then broke down everything else bit by bit. His voice, his speech, and his manner altered to soothe his Anglo business contacts while he tore what he wanted from them. He felt his success stemmed from his understanding of the Anglo mind, and the idea that the only way to beat them was to get under their skin. For him, it had worked. Edd Villaveda was Hannibal Striker as far as the hundreds who worked for him were concerned and if he wanted them to call him H. A., they'd call him H. A.

"I'm telling you, H. A.," Sweetboy warned once he had regained his seat and a plate of fresh fruit was placed before him, "Callahan should be taken care of now."

"No, no," Striker said after wrapping his mouth around a succulent strawberry soaked in rum. "We watch and wait. The San Francisco inspector is our chance to trace Tucker's team to its source. If Callahan simply gives the widow and family his condolences and goes home, all the better. But if he starts making trouble, we may discover the brains behind Tucker's arrest record. It is worth the patience."

Striker devoured a piece of pear, a half a peach, and an apricot before speaking again. "What I can't understand is why the inspector waited until now to follow up Tucker's death. Whatever could have led him to San Antonio?"

Sweetboy's expression was the picture of innocence as he systematically ripped open an apple with a steak knife. "I'm sure I don't know," he said.

Five

"Everything's big in Texas!" the slushy voice boomed in Harry's ear. "And so's the city. The tenth biggest city in the whole United States. We're bigger than Boston. We're bigger than Pittsburgh. We're bigger than all those piss-ass Eastern cities!"

Everytime the slurred voice mangled a word with "s" in it, a shower of spittle escaped from between the man's lips. By the time he had surfed through Pittsburgh and piss-ass, Harry's ear felt like the Mississippi basin. But even with the drunken drizzle, Harry would have had a hard time moving away from the man. The Four Ponies Bar was packed and he had to keep his eye on the back booth.

"We've got barrios filled with wetbacks," the drunk went on. "Half a million of 'em! We've got soldier boys. Fifty thousand of 'em on four bases! We've got the San Antonio River. We've got the Passeo . . . the Passeo . . ."

"Paseo del Rio," Harry completed for him, feeling like his ear was turning into a prune.

"Yeah, thass it," mumbled the drunk. "Everything's

big in Texas. And that's the way I like 'em. Big! You know what I mean? Big! I like 'em *big!*"

The drunk laughed hysterically over his weak metaphor. Harry thought it time to get rid of the guy. If he kept up his sodden spiel the boys in the back booth might take notice.

"You want another beer?" Harry asked the drunk.

"Sure!" the drunk responded immediately. "Gimme another brew! C'mon, give it to me!"

"There's a big, cold can of Golden State beer outside for you," said a smiling Harry. "Go on and get it."

"Golden State? All right!" cried the drunk struggling off his stool. "Thass better than Fosters. Thass better 'n Coors. Golden State, thass the beer for me." The drunk shouldered his way through the ample crowd of cowboys and Mexicans. "Clear my plate for Golden State!" was the last thing Harry heard him cry before he was swallowed up by the smoke and the crowd.

There was plenty of both in the Four Ponies on that Friday night. It had been a hard week for everybody, including Harry. He had spent his time commuting between the Ramada Inn room where he was staying and Peter Nash's cellar where the cop conspiracy was planned. Harry liked the cellar better. His hotel room was like most moderately priced hotel rooms; long, beige, dull, with beds that were almost as wide as they were long. And neither length was really enough to rest his tall frame comfortably.

The cellar was low, cool, and interesting. The floor was uneven, dirty concrete, the walls were dark stones swimming in white plaster, and the corners held webby condominiums of strange-looking bugs. But the most interesting thing about the cellar was what went on there. Every night a parade of incognito police officers would traipse through and get orders from ex-deputy Nash.

Nash, Harry discovered, was a brilliant strategist. He moved every officer in exactly the right arrangement to make a noose around his target's neck. One by one, Nash had been marking Striker's underlings for arrest and probable conviction. While most of the sentences for these crimes had been minor and bail was produced almost immediately in all cases, the constant harassment and annoyance factor must have been driving the Mexican businessman crazy.

Tonight was the night for Glen Thurston, Striker's kickback specialist. It was the first step in the new campaign to change Callahan into a thorn that would be driven into Striker's side. Once it started smarting enough, Nash was sure Sweetboy Williams would be sent out. After that Harry would go home either on a plane or in a pine box.

The San Francisco-based detective watched the back booth through the mirror behind the bar. Seated there were Thurston, a chunky, blondish hunk, and two of his kickback pals. The fourth was the outwardly affable owner of the bar. Harry saw he was doing his best to pal it up with the gang. The dozens of beer bottles and half-eaten plates of Italian food were evidence enough of that.

But Harry saw the nervousness under the owner's pleasant manner. Harry knew the owner knew why the Striker boys were here. If it wasn't for a payoff, then it was for the perks that came with being affiliated with power. Thurston and his friends were having the time of their lives, secure in the knowledge that Striker's name was enough to get them anything they wanted.

Things hadn't changed much from the twenties, Harry decided. Then it was called "protection" or "insurance." Buy your booze from me or cut me in for some of the gravy and the Ninetieth Panzergrenadier Division won't fall on your grandmother. Only today, the system was much more civilized. If I throw a lot of income your way, you throw me back some. It was still illegal and it was still thievery, but the kickbacker figured it was worth his while.

That is, he figured it was worth it until Striker and company got their claws into him. Then the kickbacks had to keep coming whether the orders got larger or not. So it had to be all smiles, spaghetti, and sauce from the bar owner or the Ninetieth Panzergrenadier Division would return.

Callahan sat, waiting for his cue. Everything had been set up perfectly. The money was set to change hands tonight. While the cops had not been ordered to set up a stake-out or surveillance, Nash arranged for two "unbought" officers to "just happen to be in the area." Another off-duty cop would just happen to be on the scene when the cash changed owners. It was Harry's job to make sure things didn't get out of hand. And if they did get out of hand, make sure that no one got away.

During the Tucker time in office, it was much easier, but now things had to be done unofficially. The arrests had to be made "by coincidence." Harry marveled at the things he got himself into. He was the muscle man in the operation. An operation that took police work out of the police's hands. For all intents and purposes, Peter Nash was declaring war on all the cops on the take with Harry being set up as the scapegoat. Long after Callahan had broken up the "Vigilante Cop," he was the prime ingredient in another one.

Thurston's dinner was finished. Harry saw the fat cat push his plate away. The place was packed with noisy, happy drinkers. The jukebox was blaring David Allan Coe's "Willie, Waylon and Me." The two pinball machines were going strong. Guys were huddled around the two video games; "Space Invaders," and "Asteroids." The cigarette, cigar, and pipe smoke had gotten as thick as Tennessee fog. It was 11:15 P.M., so it was unlikely that the place would get any busier.

If any green were going to dance across the table into Thurston's lap, it was going to dance now.

Harry was glad he had checked the place out earlier. It was a moderately sized watering hole, much like Tanya's place in his home town. The front door opened to a coat rack and a small, plastic partition. To the right of the partition were tables, a phone, and rest rooms, occasionally interrupted by potted cactus plants. To the left was the bar, flanked on both sides by the entertainment machines: pinball, video, and the jukebox.

In back of both these sections was a separate small dance hall, complete with a fenced-off section where a live band would play, more tables, a walk-in refrigerator for excess booze, and a closed-off kitchen.

The dance hall itself was closed off tonight because

the band that usually played on Fridays had a sick drummer. So instead of a few musicians and boogieing dancers, the hall was filled with crates, casks, and empty beer bottles.

The only way out of the room besides the entrance was a door between the fridge and the kitchen. It led to a back porch which led to a back yard. The back yard was fenced in on three sides, leaving an open space to the right of the porch.

To the left of the roadside bar was a business-machines shop and to the right was a truck loading depot. To drown out the sound of trucks on the move, the Four Ponies turned the pinball sound effects and the jukebox's volume way up high. Screaming your head off was common practice at the bar.

At the moment, the bar's owner was using the universal sign language of green paper. Harry saw the cash flash in the mirror even before the off-duty cop playing one of the video games did. Harry slowly swung around, slipped off the stool, and started shouldering his way toward the back.

He saw the off-duty cop staring intently at the "Asteroids" screen. Stupidly, he had agreed to play another patron. Not only was the extra man blocking some of the cop's line of sight, it made the officer too intent on the game. He seemed more interested in winning than paying attention to Thurston.

Harry looked back to the table. Thurston slid his hand over the wad of money and drew it toward the edge of the table. In a few seconds it would be over the lip and as far as any of the straight cops were concerned, gone for good. Harry glanced back at the off-duty officer. He was cursing his luck as a video-created hunk of rock destroyed the video ship he was piloting. Then he patiently waited for his score to appear.

Harry didn't know whether to jump the table or smack the cop on the side of the head. No wonder Striker was able to get control of the city, Callahan marveled. With cops like these, Nash needed all the help he could get.

After a millisecond's deliberation, Harry decided to

hit the table. Thurston's hand had palmed the cash and was just about to slip it into his coat when an iron-hard grip latched onto his wrist, squeezed like a boa constrictor, and pulled the money hand out for all to see.

It was Harry's right hand that gripped Thurston's. In Harry's left hand was the off-duty cop's collar. With the money held somewhere between Thurston's chin and the eggplant parmigiana, Harry pulled the cop until his thighs were bouncing off the table edge and his eyes were bouncing from face to face.

"Glen Thurston," said Harry, "I'd like you to meet a San Antonio police officer. Officer, this is Mr. Thurston." Harry looked from one man to the other until the full implications of the situation were obvious to both. "I hope you two will be very happy together," he finished, opening his hands and moving behind the cop. "Read him his rights, asshole," Harry instructed.

Glen Thurston had no intention of waiting around to hear them. With a roar befitting a man of his size, he placed his hands on the seat of his chair, lifted his legs, and kicked over the heavy wooden table.

The edge of the circular furniture came down on the cop's toes while the top section pushed against his lower legs. The off-duty officer fell forward and sideways at the same time, pain rocketing up his limbs. The bar owner sat aghast as the three Striker representatives went every which way but loose.

Harry was there to make sure they didn't get loose. The guy to Thurston's right came straight at Callahan. In no mood to discuss anything, Harry made sure the man met his right fist head-on. The guy to Thurston's left slid out from behind the felled table and slipped behind the partition between the bar and the rest rooms.

This partition, which stretched from one end of the room to the other was dotted with openings so the bartender could make sure no one skipped out on his check. Through one of these openings, the guy to Thurston's left poked the barrel of a snubnose gun.

Harry didn't wait to see who it might be pointed at. He ripped out his own gun, which was anything but snubnose, and shot right through the partition.

A hole the size of which was usually attributable to a shotgun blast appeared in the partition as the guy to Thurston's left flew backward in the company of tiny, spinning shards and streams of his own blood. His snub-nose spun in the air like a yo-yo at the apex of its flight, then dropped to the ground.

Harry pivoted toward Thurston himself. The kick-back master was pushing his way toward the dance hall. Thanks to the man's efforts and the sight of Harry's Magnum, a clear line was created between the inspector and the fleeing hoodlum. Harry pointed his gun at Thurston's back and was just about to say "halt," when the slush-talking drunk wavered into the line of fire.

"You lied to me," he moaned to Harry. "I looked and I looked, but there was no brew outside."

Cursing, Harry pulled his gun barrel up, threw himself forward, and bowled the drunk over with a sweeping body block. The amazed drunk thought he was flying until he landed amid the broken table, the broken dishes, the extra macaroni, and the cringing off-duty police officer.

Harry entered the dance hall in time to dodge a rain of beer bottles. Thurston was marking his escape with any box he could grab and throw behind him. Harry crouched to the side of the entrance and took aim again. This time he was able to call out "halt" without any interruptions.

Thurston reacted to the pronouncement by leaping behind a silver cask of beer and clawing at his waistband. That particular hand motion usually meant one thing to Harry; the alleged perpetrator was going for a weapon.

Acting on instinct, Harry's finger tightened on the Magnum's trigger. He immediately loosened his trigger finger for two reasons. First, he remembered that he was not shooting on home turf at a local scumbag. Usually that reason was not sufficient for Harry to let someone shoot back at him, but the second reason he didn't shoot was the more important and the more pressing. Namely, Harry didn't know whether the keg Thurston was huddled behind was full or empty.

If empty, Harry's bullets would go through like they went through almost everything else. But if it was full and under pressure, it could explode with the force of a frag grenade, sending hunks of sharp metal and gallons of beer everywhere. Under normal circumstances, Harry might have tried it, but these weren't normal circumstances. He was fighting in front of an innocent crowd and had no personal cover.

Before Thurston could bring his own gun up and aim, Harry threw himself from the room entrance into the kitchen by way of the rectangular ordering window. He slid across the Formica counter and dropped to the floor. Punctuating his landing were the sounds of two gunshots and the wholesale stampede of the bar's patrons toward the exits.

Harry hazarded a look through the ordering aperture he had jumped through. Thurston kicked over his keg cover at that very moment, charging for the rear door like the Schlitz Malt Liquor bull. He fired his gun as he went, slapping lead all around the kitchen.

Callahan ducked down while calculating Thurston's speed. As soon as he thought the guy had reached the rear door, he shot diagonally through the kitchen door. His aim was good but his timing was a smidge off. The bullet punched a hole midway up the kitchen door and blasted outside, narrowly missing both Thurston's back and the swinging back door.

Immediately afterward Harry was up and out the kitchen door himself, almost tripping over the beer keg Thurston had kicked aside. After noticing that the kickback man was still hustling across the back porch trying to find a way out of the yard, Harry hefted the metal cask up. It was empty. He carried it with him as he cautiously neared the back door.

He stood to one side, his Magnum held high and the beer keg held low. He looked back at the barroom. What patrons were left were staring at him from behind furniture. The only noise was of the off-duty cop groaning in pain from his squashed toes.

Harry looked outside. The back yard was empty. The loading lights from the truck stop next door bathed the area in a humid yellow gleam. Combined with the dark blue of the night, it made the shadows slightly green.

Harry stepped outside. He saw no human figure and he heard nothing. Harry looked to the right. The open part of the porch looked invitingly escapable. Harry shuffled in that direction for a moment, then stopped. He looked down. He thought about the fact that the porch was mounted about six feet off the ground. He thought about all the empty space between the dirt and the boards he was standing on.

Then he silently lowered the beer keg to the porch floor on its side. He placed the sole of his shoe against it and pushed. The keg slowly rolled toward the right edge of the porch.

Two seconds after it started rolling, bullet holes started appearing from underneath. As it lazily drifted to the right, gun reports would mingle with the sound of lead popping through and inside the oblong cask. As Harry had figured, Thurston was underneath the porch, shooting what he thought was a stalking policeman.

As soon as Thurston thought his stalker was dead, he himself fled. He raced out from under the porch toward the right and headed for the front of the bar and his parked car. Putting his weapon away, Harry ran over to the hole-ridden keg, picked it up, and threw it after the running man.

The fairly heavy metal cask bounced off the back of Thurston's head with a noise that was reminiscent of the sound the gong made at the beginning of a J. Arthur Rank film or throughout a Chuck Barris TV game show. Thurston's head jutted forward, then the rest of his body followed. The kickback man did a forward somersault through the air, landed heavily on his back, and lay still.

"I tell you there's nothing we can do about it," complained Sheriff Strughold in a voice mixing pride with pleading. "The gun was legally registered, the final arrest was made by a duly authorized officer of the law . . . there's absolutely nothing we can charge him with."

"Do you mean to say," H. A. Striker began, his voice mixing patience with displeasure, "that an out-of-state inspector throws a beer keg on one man's head, assaults another, kills the third, and shoots up a night spot, and he hasn't broken the law?"

"The owner isn't pressing charges," the Sheriff answered unhappily. "Every single witness backs up Callahan's plea of self-defense. Besides, its being handled by the homicide and D.A.'s office. There was nothing I could hold him on."

Hannibal Striker and Mitch Strughold stewed in the company of two bodyguards and two deputies at an outside cafe along the Paseo del Rio, the river Harry had mentioned to the drunk. It was a two and a half mile section of the San Antonio river dotted with shore-bound shops and eateries as well as floating vehicles for sight-seeing and entertainment. The six powerful men sat around a square table right at the water's edge.

On either side of them were trees that had strung lights reaching from branch to branch. It was a festive location and a beautiful Texas morning. It was a nice day to plan a vengeful counterattack.

The river was only about sixty feet wide and rarely more than twenty feet deep. Across the river from the half-dozen plotters was a walking area, often interrupted by stairways that led to stone bridges that spanned the water. On the bridge closest to the restaurant stood Harry Callahan. He watched as Striker and company talked.

He was wearing a new gray pair of pants which he had bought his first day in. It went well with his light brown jacket, the one he always wore, the light-green, button-down shirt and the maroon tie. Mrs. Nash was nice enough to take his other clothes to the wash today. She said she had to do the kids' laundry anyway.

Harry stood on the scenic bridge, looking at the lovely city, tranquil waters, and quaint restaurant, and felt depressed. He felt depressed because both Mrs. Nash and Hannibal Striker looked exactly like he thought they would. Mrs. Nash was pretty. She was small, brunette, and looked like Mary Ann on "Gilligan's Island." The word to describe her was perky. Striker, on the other hand, was tan-colored and calculatingly handsome. His face was wide, his cheekbones were high, and he was dressed as only money can dress you. His entire appearance was professionally slick. The word to describe him was oily.

Harry didn't like the idea of getting caught between those two people. Because when someone like him got caught between people like them, it was always the pretty, perky one who got hurt, no matter what happened. Even if Harry was to pull out his gun right there and then and put a bullet between Striker's eyes, somehow the pain would reach Carol Nash.

No, Harry didn't much like the situation he was in. But he liked men who killed honest sheriffs in front of their families, then kidnapped, raped, and murdered girls named Candy even less.

Harry marched across the bridge, down the steps, and toward Striker's table.

While he walked, he had to admit to himself that he had been surprised to find a message from Striker waiting at the Ramada Inn when he had returned from the police station. If nothing else, the Mexican-American businessman worked fast. The message asked Harry if he would be so kind as to join Striker for an informal breakfast the following day. That's exactly how he put it; to quote: "would you be so kind. . . ." As soon as Harry read that, he knew he was in for an oily time. For some reason, he just didn't like people to cover over their heritage with gloss. To Harry, it was like an Englishman learning a Bronx accent or a guy like him wearing a tuxedo on duty. It was so obviously false that it soon became an uncomfortable situation where someone had to mention it sooner or later.

Striker's reaction to Callahan's appearance fell right into Harry's estimation of the man. He looked up, made a quick, whispered note of Harry's approach to the others, then leaned back, smiled, and folded his hands together over his chest. What was he trying to do? Show off his expensive manicure?

"Ah, Inspector Callahan," Striker said. "How good of you to come." It figures he'd say it like that, Harry thought as he came to a stop before the one smiling face and the five wary, furtive ones. "Please be seated," Striker went on, waving to a plain, black chair to his left.

Harry checked the positioning. The empty chair was between Striker and one of his bodyguards. The other bodyguard was sitting to the businessman's right, next to the water's edge. The sheriff was sitting between his two deputies—the same guys who frisked Harry at the airport—across the table. Harry pulled back the seat and sat down.

"I hope you don't mind that we started without you," Striker said. "I was afraid you might be a bit late, seeing that you had such a busy night."

The evening had been a big success as far as Nash was concerned and a fiasco as far as Callahan was. He still had great faith in the ex-deputy's planning, but none at all in the straight cops' implementation. No matter how honest these guys were, they were still worried about their jobs. One too many successful Nash operations and their superiors on-the-take would get suspicious. That kind of pressure would take the edge off of any law officer. Besides, to most lawmen, Striker's brand of graft was common and accepted knowledge. The fact that he had Tucker killed only made most of the honest men want to keep that much farther away from him.

"No big deal," Harry said quietly. Only he knew it was a big deal. Callahan had hoped he could stay in the woodwork a bit longer to get the lay of the land. The fact that he had done most of the work last night put him in the spotlight. Now there could be no doubt as to Harry's purpose in San Antonio.

The expressions on everyone's face but Striker's mirrored Harry's thought. He felt like Custer sitting down with the Bull Run Indians. Or, to put it more aptly, given his location, Davy Crockett sitting down to lunch with the Mexican army.

"Anything we can get you?" Striker inquired, taking the lunch metaphor a little further. "Juice? Steak and eggs? A little melon, perhaps?"

"No, thanks," said Harry.

"Very well," Striker said, dabbing his lips with a napkin. "Then let's get started, shall we?" Striker continued without waiting for any kind of response from anyone. "Inspector Callahan, I'm a businessman. What's good for business is good for me, and what's good for me is good for San Antonio. The city's fathers and I have an understanding. We both like to see the city grow and prosper. We like to see a smoothly running machine. You can understand that, can't you?"

Striker's voice was unctious, lecturing, and slightly condescending. Harry wasn't bothered by it in the least. In fact, he was expecting it. He was comforted by the fact that the businessman was so easy to read. And since the businessman was posturing, Harry figured it would be best to play out his preassigned role as well.

"Yeah, I can understand that," he said. "And anything that gets in the machine's way is crushed, huh?"

Striker's reaction was smooth and full of mock-hurt. "Now why would you say a thing like that?"

Harry shrugged. "I felt it was expected of me."

That took the businessman aback. He realized then that it wasn't just another dumb cop he was dealing with. So deciding, he got down to hard cases.

"There are several ways I can deal with you, Inspector Callahan," he continued in the same light tone. "I could buy you off or I could get rid of you. Which would you suggest?"

Harry had to hand it to him. If nothing else, Striker was damn sure of his position in the world. Harry figured it was about time to shake him off his perch.

"You can't do either," Callahan replied drily. "You can't pay me off if I don't take the money and you don't have enough time to frame me. And the only way you can get rid of me is to send the hired help out to put on the muscle. And that's just what I'm waiting for."

Sheriff Strughold gave voice to what Striker's expression seemed to say. "W—w—what?"

Harry continued after glancing sardonically at the stunned Sheriff. "I'll tell you the truth, Villaveda. I'm completely disinterested in your tragic attempts to An-

89

glosize yourself. I also don't give a shit about your machine or your fucking city. All I'm doing is answering an invitation."

Striker's tan face was infused with purple. His knuckles grew white on the marble tabletop, and his body almost vibrated in rage. His two bodyguards took his near case of apoplexy as a cue for action.

As the one on Striker's left began to rise, Harry slumped down in his chair, reached under the table with his right leg, hooked his toe under the other bodyguard's chair, and pulled. The chair tipped backward, sending the second bodyguard headfirst into the river.

Sitting up, Harry then reached between the first bodyguard's clutching hands, wrapped his own strong hand around the man's tie, then stood up and swung forward at the same time. The bodyguard, off balance from trying to rise and grab Harry, lost his footing and was thrown across the table and into the river, scattering cutlery as he went.

Immediately after the two splashes subsided, Harry stepped back, both hands innocently raised to his shoulder level. The two deputies were going to leap up anyway until Striker raised one of his own hands. The policemen became still lifes halfway out of their seats.

Striker breathed deeply through his nose and exhaled out his mouth as the deputies slowly regained their seats. Harry realized the businessman wasn't going to speak by the time both bodyguards had sputtered back onto dry land. The inspector turned to leave as Striker slowly lowered his hand. The five other men watched Callahan go.

"H. A., we should've . . . !" Strughold sputtered until Striker raised his hand again. They all kept silent until Harry had crossed the bridge and disappeared into a white building on the other side.

"It's fine," Striker soothed, regaining his composure. "It's all right. We've learned a lot today. This entire regrettable incident has given me an idea."

Striker was a little less civilized when he confronted Sweetboy Williams later that afternoon. *"Stupido!"* he screamed, slapping himself on the forehead. "I ignored the mess you made of the Tucker hit. I've ignored your eccentricities, your minor idiosyncrasies, but this is too much—too much! All those things you said were mistakes were not mistakes, were they? *Were they?*"

"You hired me because I was the best, right?" Sweetboy answered calmly. "The Tucker thing worked because I meant it to work. The Callahan thing could work as well."

"As well?" Striker exploded in amazement. "As well? Bodies littering an amusement park? A rape-murder in Los Angeles?"

"It got him here, didn't it?"

"Who wants him here?" Striker shouted, his face getting purple again. "Not me. It was *your* aggravated sense of wild West fantasy that hatched this showdown idea. Callahan said he was answering an invitation. It was your invitation. Your invitation has left a trail of blood that has led to me!"

"Don't worry about it," Williams complained. "Callahan's a renegade. There's nothing official he can do. And once he's out of the way, things'll get back to normal."

"Normal?" Striker asked the ceiling. "Normal? A dead San Francisco inspector? San Francisco investigators crawling all over the place? San Francisco chiefs pressuring San Antonio chiefs? That's normal?"

"Callahan's a renegade," Williams repeated. "A rogue. A maverick. He's got no friends, and his reputation is dicey. His Frisco superiors will probably be glad he finally bought it."

"No," Striker said flatly, sitting behind his large oak desk in his Spanish-style office. "You will not kill Inspector Callahan. You will go nowhere near Inspector Callahan. I shall accept the opinion that your luring him to San Antonio was done with what you felt were my best interests in mind. I grant you that he was Tucker's friend and the most likely man to seek revenge, but this must not turn into a high-noon shoot-out.

"No," Striker repeated. "There is another, more

effective way of eliminating Inspector Callahan from the scene. I shall ask for your cooperation in this matter. Do I have it?"

"Yes," Williams said immediately, rising from the thick beige couch in front of the desk.

"Then you will not approach Inspector Callahan in any way, is that understood?"

"Yes."

"Good." Striker leaned back in the tall, brown, padded chair. "I will consider a little time off for you. A vacation. A reward, if you will, for a job well done. All right?"

"Yes," Williams said for a third time, his expression empty, his eyes looking over Striker's head.

"Very well. That's all for now."

Williams left quickly and quietly. Striker stared after him as the automatic door slid back into place. Then the businessman looked around his inner sanctum. The walls here, like the walls elsewhere in the mansion, were decorated with antique weapons. The ceiling was low and lined with gnarled crossbeams. The rest of the interior was furnished with a Spanish motif. The thick sliding door was detailed with sculpture. The beige walls were hand-stippled. The only window in the room was the large one behind Striker, outfitted with bulletproof, one-way glass so he could see the grounds but the guards and the rest of his staff couldn't see him.

Striker turned to gaze out that window. He seemed to stare through the beautifully kept flora and the various animals he let roam on the grounds. He thought about Sweetboy Williams. It had been a very touchy thing, he knew, and he felt that the assassin realized it as well. The only thing between Williams and immediate execution was Striker's attitude. For while the weapons on the wall were ancient, the weapons hidden in the desk were anything but.

It was only Williams' past accomplishments that saved him. The hitman hadn't stepped out of line until now. But it was enough. Striker knew he couldn't trust Sweetboy as he had in the past. The businessman mused over the day's two meetings. The Callahan question was already on its way toward being answered. And through that, Striker felt sure he could eradicate the people behind Tucker once and for all.

But the Williams question was still open. Striker thought about the assassin's recent actions and reactions. He knew about the taxi cab reconnaissance at the airport. He had given Williams plenty of time to admit it, but the hitman had remained silent, choosing instead to inform Striker of the out-of-date cop car through another employee. The number had not been enough. He had needed Williams to follow the vehicle and identify the drivers. Instead, the assassin had collected some information about Callahan, and Striker had found the car in question at the police junkyard.

Striker pondered it all. He decided that he would have to terminate Williams' employment quite soon. But first things first. Harry Callahan would have to be eliminated.

Six

The locale was cheery. It was time for the annual Alamo Stadium Rodeo. The crowd was cheery. Among the roaring masses that were delighting in the assembled cowboys' antics were Peter Nash and his family. The weather was cheery. The sun shone bright on the Stadium and its sparkling surroundings, Brackenridge Park, the San Antonio River, and the Hemis-Fair Plaza.

The only thing that wasn't cheery was Harry Callahan. He felt the heavy weight of a cross-hair sight across his face all the time. He didn't like the crowd, he didn't like the noise, and he didn't like the stake-out.

"Don't worry," Nash had said. "Everything is tightly planned."

"As tight as the Four Ponies Bar?" Harry had asked.

"Tighter. Come on, don't worry, Harry, we're using only experienced officers this time. The whole thing will go down smooth as silk. You'll see."

But Harry had made his living worrying. It kept him

on his toes and above ground. "I don't like Carol and the kids being here."

"Come on," Nash said again. "I take them to the Rodeo every year. We'll be three people amid tens of thousands!"

Even so, Harry didn't like it. The whole situation had come together too easily. Word had gotten around that another Striker payoff was going down at the Rodeo. That made sense. It was one of the biggest civic events that occurred all year. It would be natural that Striker would skim off some extra cream. But the way the rest of the plan fell into place bothered Callahan.

He was to backstop Officer Henry Lieber, a by-the-book veteran who was set to catch Jack Foster, another Striker employee, in the act of payoff. That, too, was fine. What really worried Harry was that a huge stadium with thousands of screaming fans was a perfect place to payoff an out-of-town inspector. Harry kept about a tenth of his attention on Lieber and Foster, and ninety percent of his instincts were scanning the area for a Sweetboy.

To lower the risk of a back attack, Harry positioned himself against a solid concrete wall near the stables. He was watching the main stadium office from across an open area lined with animal enclosures. In the middle of the oblong space were heaps of straw and a wagon or two. Beyond that was a driveway leading to the stadium grounds flanked by paths into both sides of the stands.

Harry had been busying himself at that end of the open space for about fifteen minutes as off-duty officer Lieber worked his nonchalant way toward the office. The plan was to wait until Foster went inside the office, then they'd both move in to catch him in the act of receiving a kickback.

According to Nash's information, Foster was late. That didn't bother Harry a bit. If he had his druthers, Foster wouldn't show at all, so Harry could wait until the rodeo ended and everyone went home before leaving himself.

Lieber signaled that he would check up the road a bit to see if Foster was coming. Harry, preoccupied, signaled back in the affirmative. He was so intent on other things that he didn't notice the look of honest regret that passed over Lieber's face.

It didn't take long for Lieber to disappear and a gang of youths to start ambling into the stable space.

Harry's expression didn't change, but his blood chilled for a moment, then picked up circulatory speed throughout his body. It was looking more and more like a setup, all right, but not the kind he was expecting.

In came the Mexican who had slashed his pants at the airport. Next came the kid who had stuffed his underwear. He recognized them all. It was the exact same group who accosted his luggage. Finally in sauntered Tattoo. As soon as he appeared, Harry toyed with the notion that Tattoo was Sweetboy. It didn't seem likely, but the inspector wasn't about to take chances. He placed his right hand inside his coat and moved forward to meet them.

The gang spread out across the enclosure, taking up what seemed to be preplanned positions near the middle of the stable space. They lined its equator, effectively blocking any route of escape. Harry saw that Tattoo was wearing a sleeveless T-shirt and a dark green vest. As the inspector neared, Tattoo nonchalantly opened his vest to expose his torso.

"See?" he asked Harry. "No weapons."

"No guns," said the Mexican, unbuttoning his shirt.

"No knives," said another kid, pulling off his jacket.

"No clubs," said a third, turning all the way around with his arms out.

"No weapons of any kind," said a kid in the back, pulling down his pants and giving Callahan a quick moon.

"So it would be murder if you shot any one of us with that big gun of yours," Tattoo hastened to add.

Harry looked everyone over. Almost all the kids were wiry. One or two were heavily muscled. All of them looked like products of manual labor. There didn't seem to be a weak link among them. Even if there had been, the enclosure wasn't wide enough and there were too many of them to barrel through, then outrun them. Harry looked down. On all their feet were the customary pointed Texas cowboy boots. Whatever happened, Harry thought, he wouldn't let them get him on the ground.

He also wouldn't throw the first punch. What he would do was play a sort of pedestrian chicken. He started to speed up his walk as he moved toward Tattoo. The kid stood his ground until Harry was almost right on top of him. It then became quite clear that Harry wasn't going to stop and there was no way Tattoo was going to stop him by just standing there.

At the last second, Tattoo, pivoted, twisted, and got out of Harry's way. At the same time he hopped in back of the inspector, jumped up, and swung his arm at the back of Harry's head.

Harry ducked and swung backward. The kid's arm shot through empty air, pulling him forward. He collided midway with Harry's elbow, pushing him back. Tattoo's mouth opened to release an explosive exhalation and some of his lunch. Then he took a step backward, lost his footing, fell through the air for three feet, and landed flat on his back.

Even before Tattoo stopped choking on his puke and yelled for the others, the rest of the gang had taken Harry's action as a declaration of war.

Harry kicked the first kid to his left. His foot, connecting with the kid's solar plexus, braced him to turn toward the right and catch the first kid there in the nose. Then they started coming from all directions.

Harry did some fast calculations. He had taken out three and only one of those had no chance of coming back. Tattoo was already finding his feet. So that meant at least six kids to take out in a non-permanent fashion.

Someone grabbed him around the waist from the front. He clubbed the guy with both fists on the back of the neck. Two down. But the tackle had pushed him back into the waiting fists of one of the muscular boys. He felt one first graze his ear and the other smack solidly into the back of his neck. He only felt the pain while already twisting around, the side of his palm making a whirring noise in the air. It landed against the attacking boy's ear.

The kid's head swung away as Harry felt a boot smash into the small of his back. The pain and power of that blow was amazing, but it was that very realization that kept him from going down. Even as he was flying forward from the force of the flying kick, Harry somehow found his footing. The horror of what those same boots could do to him while he was helpless on the ground was enough to keep him upright. With an incredible effort he stumbled, found his footing, spun, and delivered a devastating punch to the face of the Mexican.

The kid had run after him when it seemed certain he would fall. The Mexican's momentum was too strong to stop when Harry miraculously turned and punched. Even though the Mexican's hands were up, Harry's fist sank into his face, sending a halo of blood in all directions. That was three down.

It was enough for Harry. He enjoyed exercise as much as the next guy, but he saw no sport in playing punching bag. Before the next kid could charge, Harry pulled out his Magnum, pointed it at the ceiling, and pulled the trigger. The effect was instantaneous. All the stabled animals went crazy, the gang stopped dead in its tracks, and the office door opened to reveal Sheriff Mitch Strughold and his deputies.

Everybody except Harry was smiling.

"Man," said Tattoo in a husky, broken voice, "that guy's crazy."

"Yeah," chimed in another kid, "he just started beating up on us for no reason at all."

"Look what he did to Frank and Manwell," choked a third.

"Wall, wall, wall," said the sheriff, his hands back in his gun belt. "Looks like we have a dangerous fugitive here, boys. I think y'all better keep yer guns on him while I read him his rights."

The sheriff was more than happy to do more than read Harry his rights. He was happy to take his Magnum away from him. He was happy to cuff Harry's hands in front of him. He was happy to personally herd Harry to his car. He was happy to join Harry in the back seat. And he was happy to gloat.

"Oh, my, my, my, y'all really shoulda stayed home," the sheriff laughed. "Everythin' was goin' just fine until you showed up."

Strughold smiled, chuckled, and all but hopped up and down in the seat as the car wound its way out of the stadium. Harry could understand where some of Mitch's mirth was coming from, but he couldn't fathom why the sheriff was acting like it was Christmas. He didn't have to wait long to find out.

"Had to play the hero, din't ya?" the sheriff cackled. "Had to face Thurston yerself, huh?"

"What are you babbling about?" Harry asked tiredly.

"Babblin'? Babblin'? Why, that's a hell of a thing to say! And you bein' the man who blew Tucker's system to shit!"

Callahan had a funny way of reacting to trouble. Rather than becoming upset, morose, or despondent, he got crafty. As soon as Sheriff Strughold delivered that last bombshell, Harry was already trying to figure a way out. In the meantime, he had to keep the idiot talking.

"What do you mean?" he asked, allowing some doubt to creep into his voice.

"I mean jes that!" the sheriff chortled, holding his sides. "I mean you couldn'ta known that Thurston was going to be there the other night, so somebody had ta tell ya. So all of a sudden, we knew there was somebody tellin' Tucker too. Then all we hadda do was find out who and git you outta the way!"

Strughold took a moment to slap his two deputies on the back. They joined in with his laughter as the car turned on to the road outside the stadium.

"Wtll, you haven't got me yet," Harry said, bringing the Sheriff's attention back to him. "This thing will never hold up in court."

"The hell it won't!" Strughold announced. "The only witnesses you got is those kids an' they'll say anythin' we tell 'em to."

"How about Officer Lieber?" Harry asked, already knowing the answer, but desperate to keep Strughold confessing.

"Hell, his pension is more important to him than the likes a' you! Once we found out he was goin' ta be the arresting officer, the rest was easy."

"How did you find out?" Harry asked, playing on the sheriff's ego. "Our plan was perfect."

"Well, ya see, that's the problem with hospitals," Strughold said cryptically. "Once you get a wounded officer into a bed, its kinda hard to keep track of all the drugs that's pumped inta 'im. Sometimes they kin be a kinda mistake, y'know? And then the officer gets a bad case of diarrhea of the mouth, if ya know what I mean."

Harry blessed the sheriff's own infection for revealing the truth. Somehow, probably very easily, Striker had gotten to the off-duty officer with the crushed toes. Pumping the guy with truth serum, or perhaps just threatening him and his family, Striker had gotten the full story as to how the Four Ponies arrest went down.

And if Striker knew how that worked, he knew that Nash was behind it.

The situation had gotten far worse than Harry expected. Given the situation, Harry wouldn't have been surprised if Striker had reserved a nasty, uncozy jail cell for him and thrown away not only the key, but the lock as well. And once he got out, he wouldn't be surprised if Nash had joined Tucker in that great courtroom in the sky and his badge was in serious jeopardy.

The latter problem didn't faze Harry in the least. His badge had been in jeopardy before. But contrary to the James Bond book and movie title of the past, you only live once. Peter Nash, not to mention his family, were in incredible danger. And if Harry was rotting behind bars, there was nothing he could do about it.

Harry looked at the three cops as the car turned onto New Graunfels Avenue, heading toward Route 81. Once the car hit the highway and picked up speed, Harry knew any escape would be that much harder. He looked around the seat for the .44 Magnum. Thankfully, Strughold was so sure of himself that he left the big gun lying next to his left thigh. In order to get it, Harry would have to reach across the sheriff's bulk.

Harry looked at the door next to him. It was locked,

naturally, and there was no door tab to let the alleged perpetrator unlock it. But Harry knew where the lock mechanism was inside the door. One high-powered bullet and the door should open. Yeah, and one punch and the sheriff should lose consciousness. And if he went fast enough the deputies should be too stunned to react. And the car should be going slow enough so when he jumped out he didn't break both arms, both legs, and most of his ribs. And if he was really good this year, he wouldn't get coal in his Christmas stocking.

Looking at it objectively, Harry knew that the only thing he had going for him was surprise. No one in his right mind would consider battling three armed cops while he had handcuffs on. And no inspector in his right mind would jeopardize his life and career to assault another officer and avoid capture. That was what Strughold was probably counting on. Both the sheriff and Striker thought that Harry would roll over and play dead rather than play with his future.

It was time to prove them wrong, Harry figured. As he twisted his wrists to see what kind of give the handcuffs had, he thought, of all things, about how the cartoon character Tweety Pie would have put it. "He don't know me very well, do he?" rocketed through Harry's mind, then he moved.

Lucky for Callahan, the sheriff decided to say something to his deputies at that very moment. So Strughold's face met Harry's clenched hands halfway up. The back of the car reverberated with a loud smacking sound, then Strughold reared back, his eyes closed. As soon as Harry felt his fists meet flesh, he pulled his arms down and grabbed the Magnum's butt.

Swinging back, he pushed the gun barrel against the door, just under the armrest and pulled the trigger. The smacking sound mingled with an earsplitting boom. The deputy in the passenger's seat saw a flash and the driver accidentally jerked the steering wheel in surprise. The car swerved, but the back door remained closed.

Callahan stared in shock just long enough to notice that the deputy in the passenger seat was turning around.

Then he reared back himself, brought his feet up, and kicked at the door with all his might.

Then it burst open. Harry's legs swung outside the swerving car. The door swung out, then bounced back. Harry met it with his shoulder as he threw the rest of his body forward. Thankfully, the surprised driver hit the brakes right after the gun went off, so the speed Harry was falling out at wasn't really a problem. What was a problem was that the cop car was well on its way toward stopping, so that the deputies could get out and decorate his body with bullet holes.

That thought did much to keep Harry moving fast. He hit the ground and rolled as the car arced away from him. The actual landing wasn't as awful as it could have been, so Harry spent his spinning time praying that another car didn't run him over. Happily for him, the street was empty because almost everyone in the area was inside Alamo Stadium.

Harry pulled himself to an abrupt stop, resting on his elbows and knees. To his delight, the Magnum was still clenched in both hands, the cop car was fifty feet down the street and still rolling, and there was an embankment nearby. He got up quickly but painfully. His left leg announced to his brain that it was wounded as his eyes focused on the police car. As he watched, the vehicle screeched to a halt and the passenger door opened. Trotting toward the side of the road, Harry pointed the Magnum at the opening door and fired. A hole ripped through the door's window, splattering glass across the road. The door closed.

Harry dived over the embankment and rolled down a grassy hill into a wooded area. Taking no time to look back, he got up and ran. He ran through the mass of cypress and oak trees, smelling the cool, comforting scent of nearby water. If his knowledge of San Antonio geography was right, he was near the river, just before it wound its way through Brackenridge Park.

Harry spied the boat basin even before he got out of the woods. His timing was terrific because just then he heard the sounds of pursuit behind him. The dock was a small one, mostly lined with sightseeing vehicles. Some were the two-person floaters where a pair made it go by cycling a riverboat-like paddle. Others were bigger flat-bed barges outfitted with rows of seats for a leisurely tour down the Paseo. But there were also one or two sleek outboard crafts built for faster speeds. Harry ran out of the tree cover toward the ships.

No one noticed the handcuffed, gun-wielding inspector until the pursuing cops started yelling. Then the innocent bystanders looked toward the racing uniformed deputies, then in the direction they were pointing. All of a sudden Harry's desperate plight became shared knowledge. Immediately thereafter everyone started getting out of the way.

A man tackled his wife and kids to get down to ground level. Groups of teenagers dived off the paddle-boats. Workers started deserting the dock *en masse* as a scuffed, bloodied, sweating man in handcuffs holding a huge revolver came running right at them. The only person who didn't move was one lone boatman holding the anchor rope from one of the motorboats. He kneeled by the craft, staring at Harry in shock.

Callahan pointed the Magnum at him. "The key!" Harry demanded. He lucked out. The guy immediately stuck his hand into his pocket and tossed him the key. Harry had to pull the gun away from the guy's head to catch it, and the guy took the opportunity to try jumping him.

Harry marveled at the guy's bravery and stupidity. Then he clubbed him on the head with the Magnum and jumped into the boat. It was an unpretentious craft with two seats, a regular wheel, and standard clutch. Harry threw his gun onto the driver's seat and rammed the key into the corresponding keyhole.

A bullet slashed through the boat's windshield. Harry pivoted, grabbed his gun, and blasted back at the two cops. They had just reached the rear of the basin. Harry's shot went in between them, but it was enough to split them up and make them dive under cover.

Callahan turned back to the boat's dash and tried to turn the key with the gun still in his hand. The barrel was too long. He turned back toward the cops and fired again to keep them down, then dropped the gun on the dash and turned the key.

The boat roared into life, but without pushing forward the clutch, it would only roar in one place. Harry realized that at about the same time the deputies did. Harry's cuffed hands were reaching for the device when another bullet splattered into the driver's seat. Another came hot on its heels, making a hole in the dash next to Harry's legs.

"Shit!" Callahan cursed, scrambling for the Magnum and slamming his back against the dashboard. He wasn't so much worried about one of the bullets hitting him as he was about one of them hitting the gas tank. He pointed the revolver with both hands and repeatedly pulled the trigger as he arched his back. His lower vertebra did the trick. It connected with the clutch and the boat jerked forward.

Just as the craft started to move, Harry's gun ran out of ammunition. The click of the hammer hitting an empty chamber was drowned out by the growl of the motor, but the deputies saw that nothing was coming out of the Magnum barrel. Harry knew he didn't have time to reload so he turned all his concentration on driving.

The deputy who had been driving saw it as a chance to peg the escaping inspector dead to rights. He raced forward along the dock, firing as he went. The bullets smacked all around Harry. He turned to see that the anchor line was still attached to both the boat's rear clasp and the pier's pylon. Harry wondered which would give out first as he pushed the clutch all the way over.

They both did. As soon as the rope grew taut, Harry poured on the speed. There was a loud twang, a tearing sound, and then the pylon cracked, the clasp flew off and the last board making up the dock dropped into the river just as the deputy stepped on it.

Both the cop's legs flew into the air, his gun went spinning into the water, and he landed heavily on his back. To add insult to injury, the metal clasp boomeranged and slapped him in the side. He howled in surprised pain as Harry sped down the river.

The other deputy jumped right over his partner and into the other motorboat. He screamed for the key as well as yelling at his dazed associate to radio for more help. The boat's key was thrown to him as the wounded cop hobbled back toward their car.

The second chase was on. Harry had traded a running race with a speedboat sprint. And he knew it wouldn't be a very long one. The Paseo del Rio was not only a very shallow river section, it was an often-interrupted one. Even casual canoeists had to cross dozens of portages to get anywhere in the city.

Harry broke open his revolver chambers, threw his gun on the dash, and dug into his pocket for one of the four auto-loaders he always carried with him. He used to carry only three, but after the homicidal Lieutenant Briggs caught him with his bullets down during the "Magnum Force" case, he had decided an extra wouldn't hurt. No one would ever completely disarm him again.

As he dug one out, he noticed his leg wound. Almost the entire left pant leg was ripped open, exposing a nasty looking cut that stretched from his lower thigh to his lower calf. It couldn't be that bad, Harry reasoned, since he could still stand on it. So deciding, he ignored it and got back to reloading his gun while steering the careening boat.

Lining up the auto-loader with the gun's chamber was child's play. Locking the cartridges in was a little harder. Every time he pushed on the auto-loader the gun would also be pushed forward. He quickly jammed the barrel against the side of the dash, then pushed the auto-loader. The bullets slid in, the auto-loader clicked and let go. Then being done, Harry wished there was some way he could shoot the handcuff chain in two.

He wished for a way all the more when he heard another bullet zing over his head. Harry turned to see a deputy in a speedboat hot on his tail. He didn't bother to shoot back. Hitting anything from a careening boat while trying to steer with handcuffs on was unlikely. Shooting a duly authorized Texas deputy was the same as committing suicide anyway. At this point in the game, Harry would settle for survival.

He ducked down in the driver's seat and concentrated all his effort on avoiding a crack-up. Coming up fast on the port side was a tourist barge lazily drifting past the sights. The deputy saw it, too, and lowered his gun. It would not do for a visitor to get croaked by a cop on the river. That gave Harry a little extra time to think.

The two motorboats rushed past the barge, sending up a double wave in their wake, which doused all the vacationers. Harry also noticed that his wake bounced off the tourist craft and splashed the following boat. It served to blind the deputy for a second. It was only a second, but that might be all he needed.

The deputy wasn't waiting. He started shooting at Harry as soon as the barge was safely past. Harry still ignored the shots. As long as the lead didn't hit him, he didn't mind it. The chance of the deputy finding his mark on the choppy seas that Harry's engine stirred up was slim. Harry's chances of escaping were just as slim. By now the wounded deputy had called in. Any second, more police cars would be roaring into the area. Harry had to get off the water.

The fugitive inspector turned a corner in the river, hearing his rotors scrape the shallow bottom. The boat sputtered and drifted for a second, but then found deeper water and surged forward again. The deputy came around the same corner wide, bumping harshly against the concrete siding. His boat waffled as well, righted, and continued the chase.

Up ahead, Harry saw what he was looking for. There was another tour barge, and, a football field beyond that, the end of the line. This section of the Paseo wound up like the shallow end of a swimming pool. The bottom was built up into a concrete landing with stairways on both sides.

Harry turned to see how far the deputy was trailing. He was glad to see he had maintained the same lead. Crouching near the edge of the boat, Harry opened up the throttle as wide as it would go, building up nearly uncontrollable speed. He rocketed by the second barge, sending up an impressive wave.

The water descended on the tourists, accompanied

by their unanimous wail. And, again, a section of the wake slapped the barge's side and swept into the other speedboat's bow. As soon as Harry saw the deputy disappear into the blue-tan liquid, he slid over the side.

Since his hand was off the clutch, the boat slowed. It slowed enough for the deputy to catch up, but not enough to stop in time for the section's end. The deputy triumphantly pulled aside the decelerating craft and leveled his pistol at an empty cockpit.

"Halt in the name of the holy fuck!" is what the deputy said as both boats screeched across the sloping end of the line. Harry's boat swerved sideways, the engine rotors slapped onto dry concrete, and the craft started flipping. The deputy hauled back on his clutch in time to avoid crashing against the embankment. Instead his boat slowed to a scraping, tortuous stop. Harry's boat kept flipping until it cracked into a stairway and bashed its hull all to hell.

Harry wouldn't have minded an explosion. The concussion, noise, and flame of one would have made a great cover for the remainder of his escape. As it was, he had to drag himself out of the river, crawl across the sidewalk, drip-dry his Magnum, and avoid the arriving squad cars without one.

It wasn't as easy, but he did it anyway.

Seven

The only noise in Boris Tucker's house was the sound of the cellar door slamming.

It was one of those thick cellar doors with a layer of sheet metal tacked up on both sides. Every once in a while those sheets would swing back lazily, then get pulled forward. There would be a small scrape and a big slam.

It was no big deal. Dotty and the kids weren't around to hear it. They had gone to stay with Dotty's mother in New Mexico until the grief passed over. The neighbors didn't hear it because the nearest one was three acres away. Boris Tucker liked privacy.

Only Harry Callahan heard it, and he didn't care. He didn't care because he was dog-tired and frustrated as a one-legged man at an ass-kicking contest. Or, to be more precise, a one-armed man at a juggling convention. He was wrapping the handcuff chain around the door bolt and slamming it shut.

And he was only doing that because he had tried everything else. Tucker hadn't been a handy man, so while Harry did find a rusted hacksaw in the cellar, he couldn't find a vise to clamp it still in. He tried using a kitchen drawer for the same purpose, but it wasn't tight enough. He tried wedging it in every hole he could find, but it didn't work.

Then he tried prying one of the links loose. It didn't work. He tried hammering the cuffs open by hitting things. It didn't work. He even seriously considered melting them open over the stove but he didn't relish char-broiled hands.

At this point, however, he didn't see how his palms could get any rawer. They were already cut, filthy, and bleeding. As a matter of fact, most of him was cut, filthy, and bleeding.

His leg had scabbed up once, only to be cut and scabbed again. It was not a pretty sight. Considering the fact that the cuts were red, his leg was white and the scabs were bluish, his left lower limb looked like the American flag. His clothes looked like they belonged to the Incredible Hulk's wardrobe after a particularly bad night. Knees and elbows torn, water and dirt combined to make his outfit look like a giant raisin ready for harvest.

As soon as he got the handcuffs broken, Harry decided he would ransack Tucker's son's room. The boy was away at college, but he was bound to have at least a pair of jeans and a work shirt Harry could use. But only after he got the fucking handcuffs off.

Harry's face was bathed in sweat. Harry was chewing his lower lip. Harry's brain was in a turmoil. Harry's existence was in a mess. His exhaustion and helplessness were getting a little much to bear.

Summing up what was left of his anger-driven strength, he wrapped the chain around the bolt again and pulled with all his might. He pulled so hard that the chain popped off the bolt before the door closed and Harry fell flat on his back on the kitchen floor.

His skull slapped the bright floor tile, sending a starblaze across his eyes. He stared at the multicolored firework display of his mind while cringing on the floor. When his vision cleared, he was lying with his legs almost

110

in the lotus position. He sat up without moving his legs. His vision clouded again and a little knife stabbed his brain a couple of times, but then the pain and the purple haze went away.

Harry found himself staring at his shoes. With his vision slightly doubled, he saw the soles of his shoes facing each other. He blinked and shook his head. His eyes then saw single again. He got to thinking about the soles of his shoes. Especially about the way they sloped inward and met the edge of the shoe heel. Then he got up and started rummaging through every kitchen drawer.

He stopped searching when he found a long piece of string. He took the string over to the kitchen table where his Magnum lay. He tied one end of the string to the trigger. He took the other end of the string and put it in his mouth. Then he took the gun and sat down on the kitchen floor, facing the cellar door.

Harry splayed his knees out until the soles of his shoes were facing each other. Held flat against each other that way, there was only a space right after the heels met. It was a triangular space that was closed off the other side by the toes of his shoe meeting. It was a space almost perfectly proportioned to a gun butt.

Harry pulled back the hammer until it clicked into place. Then he put the gun butt in between his shoes. Tightening his leg muscles effectively locked the pistol in a rubber vise. The barrel was pointing away from him, roughly centered toward the top of the cellar door. Harry stretched his hands apart as far as they would go. He reached forward until the handcuff chain was in front of the magnum barrel. Then he started eating the string.

He was sweating worse than ever now. His legs began to vibrate with the effort of keeping the gun perfectly still. He was afraid his arms would start shaking as well, making the whole proposition risky. He decided to do it as fast as possible.

The string grew taut between his teeth and the trigger. He leaned back as far as he could without moving his hands. He felt the pressure of the gun between his feet. If his feet, the gun, or his hands moved at all, he might succeed in creating the most complicated suicide ever.

His whole body was as tight as a teetotaler four vodkas later. His lips were completely off his teeth. He looked like a wolf about to devour its prey. He closed his eyes. He jerked his head back.

There was an explosion of sound. It was the intermingling of the gunshot, his own shout, and the noise of his torso and arms slamming down onto the tile. Afterwards, he heard the gun clatter to the floor as well. His legs stretched out.

He opened his eyes. He saw his right hand. It was stretched out above his head. It was still attached to his arm but it was no longer attached to his other wrist. He had done it. He had shot the chain between the cuffs.

He closed his eyes and slept.

Harry awoke. He wasn't captured. He wasn't dead. He wondered why.

Maybe Striker thought Tucker's house would be the last place Callahan would go. Maybe Sheriff Strughold was in the hospital and the regular cops didn't know Harry's connection to Tucker. Whatever the reason, Harry wasn't going to look a gift horse in the mouth. He'd examine the rest of it, maybe, but he'd leave the mouth alone.

Speaking of horses' mouths, the inside of his own felt like one. Now that the rest had cleared the cobwebs from his mind, he needed a little nourishment to clear the cobwebs from his stomach. Harry got to his feet as sprightly as he could and investigated the cupboards. He found a can of cheese ravioli, a can of ham, a quart of milk, and a bottle of orange juice. He opened them, cooked them, sliced them, poured them, drank them, and ate them all.

He was feeling better so he wandered into the son Fred's room. Fred had wanted to get away from it all, so he went to M.I.T. in Cambridge, Massachusetts. It was lucky for his family that he was a brilliant statistician, and it was lucky for Harry that he was tall. The inspector found a pair of straight-leg jeans that had their cuffs rolled up in a popular 1950s style that had come back

into fashion. With the cuffs rolled all the way back ⌐
they fit Harry.

Harry checked the rest of his clothes. Only the shirt
was salvageable. The jacket and shoes were shot to shit.
Harry discovered that a pair of Boris' old boots fit, and
one of Fred's lived-in light corduroy jackets was just
what the doctor ordered. Not only did it mask his shoulder
holster and gun effectively, the sleeves were slightly long
on him, covering the still-locked remnants of the handcuffs.
On anything but close-up examination, Harry would look
like he was wearing a watch on one wrist and a matching
bracelet on the other.

He completed the outfit with a Western belt he
found in Fred's closet. Afterwards, he searched through
Boris' closet until he found a gun-cleaning kit. He
brought it to the kitchen table and started working over
the Magnum.

Harry had just got all the sludge out of it when the
phone rang. For two rings he thought about not answering it. On the third ring he figured that not answering
might be just as incriminating as answering it. On the
fourth ring, he wondered how he could have thought that.
On the fifth ring he decided that he needed more sleep
and picked up the phone.

He didn't say hello. A breathy female voice on the
other end did. He thought it must be a wrong number or
a hooker doing a telethon until he recognized that the
breathiness didn't come from sex appeal but a lack of air
from crying.

"Carol?" he asked.

"Harry?" was the tearful reply. "Oh God, Harry!"
Carol Nash moaned.

She really didn't have to say anything after that.
Callahan had already filled in the picture for himself.
Peter had disappeared. She had called everyone she knew
to try and find out where he was. When that didn't work
she got desperate enough to search for and find his
personal book of numbers. She started at "A." It wasn't
until "T" that she made connection with Harry.

He soothed her, feeling the depression he had felt

113

before. Pretty ladies shouldn't marry cops. Pretty ladies shouldn't meet cops. Pretty ladies shouldn't need cops. But somehow, some way pretty ladies had become the prime target for the twentieth century. Whenever one got hurt, kidnapped, raped, or killed, it was front-page, indepth news. And all the coverage seemed to promote her anguish. In the 1980s, hurting pretty ladies had become a form of self-expression.

So Carol Nash was lucky. All she had was a missing husband who was probably dead. Harry's depression was displaced by dark anger; the kind Harry used to fuel his life. It was a quiet, painless rage at all the injustices of civilization rolled together. It was a dark sense of realism. A feeling of reckless capability. Harry knew he had to do something.

The game was over, the playing had stopped, no more fooling around. Dirty Harry was taking over now.

"I want him," Harry said.

Hannibal Striker was immediately struck by Callahan's similarity to Sweetboy Williams. Their approach was the same, their physicality was the same, and their capabilities were the same. The businessman was about to discover that the threat they both posed to him was the same.

Regaining a modicum of his composure, Striker tried to take control of the conversation.

"Ah, Inspector Callahan!" he said to the conference phone speaker on his desk. "It's so good to know you're still within the confines of our fair city and in one piece!"

"Can the bullshit," Harry said into the pay phone receiver. "It won't matter if you trace this call, I'll be gone by the time anyone gets here."

"Causing you difficulty is the last thing on my mind," Striker said smoothly, inwardly cursing. "I only want what's best for both of us."

"Then release Peter Nash," Harry instructed, keeping a watch all around the phone booth.

"I don't know what you mean."

"I said no bullshit," the inspector flatly stated. "Neither of us have time."

"What makes you think I—?"

"He isn't dead yet for two reasons. You need to find out how much he knows about your operation and who else knows and you need him to bait me."

"Bait you?" Striker said with the most innocence he could muster. "Why would I want to bait you?"

"Christ," Harry said angrily. "Once a wetback, always a wetback."

Striker's manner immediately changed.

"Look, you bastard, I'll make a deal—"

"I don't have to make deals with you," countered Callahan, switching ears.

"I said I was willing to make a deal!" Striker shouted into the speaker, his hands gripping the desk.

"Who gives a shit," Harry replied calmly. "You miss the point. I don't have anything to lose. I've already gone too far."

"I could get the charges dropped," Striker yelled defensively.

"I'm going to trust you?" Harry asked incredulously. "Forget it, Edd. I'll make *you* a deal."

Striker was on his feet, hollering down at the desk speaker as if it were a naughty child. "Who the hell do you think you are? This is my town! What could you possibly offer me?"

"You let Nash go and I won't kill you."

Striker's mouth dropped open. He flopped down into his seat heavily. "I don't believe this," he said plaintively.

"You've got to come out sometime," Harry said pleasantly. "I'll be there."

"You're crazy," said Striker.

"Yes, I am," Harry agreed.

Callahan waited for the inevitable. Striker would either hang up or start negotiating. Either way, Harry was still in a fight for his life.

"All right," the Mexican businessman finally said. "All right. I'll let Nash go."

"Fine," said Harry.

"But I won't let you go!" Striker exploded.

"Fine," Harry repeated.

The businessman was again taken aback by Harry's

manner. He had to sit in his big brown chair and breath deeply a few times before he was able to continue. Harry didn't mind. He expected the Mexican to be a hothead. It gave him that secure feeling that he knew with whom he was dealing. That feeling might be the difference between life and death when it came down to the inevitable confrontation.

"That means you will be brought up on charges for your full range of crimes," Striker said, trying to make Harry a bit more humble.

"Fine," Harry answered, tiredly closing his eyes. He felt like laughing. Hannibal Striker talking about crime prosecution. It was like David Dukes joining the NAACP. "I'll take my chances," he told the businessman.

"We'll meet at the Tucker house for the switch," Striker continued, becoming more decisive.

"The Tucker house?" It was Harry's turn to be taken aback.

"Don't worry," Striker told him smugly. "It's empty."

"You sure?" Harry asked cautiously. He didn't want to tip his hand, but he was interested in any details he could get to adorn Striker's statement.

Thankfully, Striker took the question as another dig at this competence. "Don't be stupid!" he shouted. "I've had it checked."

Harry nodded to himself. "Forget it," he said. "We'll meet at Brackenridge Park. The Oriental Sunken Gardens at 8:00."

"I said the Tucker house!" Striker exploded, simply trying to force his superiority on the upstart inspector.

"Meet in an empty house? Just me and your army?" Harry asked incredulously. "Don't be ridiculous," he concluded and hung up.

Striker reacted to Harry's disconnection with remarkable poise, given his reactions during the conversation. The businessman closed his mouth, leaned back, and laid the flat of his hands on the beautifully polished desk top. There was a look of calculated bemusement on his face. He was thinking.

116

Harry, too, was thinking. He was thinking about how Tucker's house could have been reported empty. He was lying flat out on the kitchen floor for hours. No one could have missed that.

Unless they wanted to.

Harry reviewed what he knew about Striker's operation. While it seemed to be a huge, far-reaching network of corruption, the same faces kept popping up. It wouldn't surprise Harry if Striker had asked Sweetboy to check out several of Callahan's possible hiding places. It would be a stupid thing to do, but Harry could see Striker doing it.

And he could see Sweetboy following the orders. Even though it was a waste of the man's murderous talents, Striker may have thought it a subtle way of displaying his own superiority. The businessman might have thought it a way of keeping Williams in line. His attitude seemed to be that "I can use anybody for anything I want."

Only that attitude had begun to come back at him with a vengeance. Harry made himself a hundred-to-one bet. Sweetboy had shown up at the Tucker house. He had seen an exhausted, beat-up, unconscious Harry. He had not wanted to challenge him unless he was at the top of his form. But he didn't want Striker to get his hands on him either. So he reported the house empty.

Harry smiled grimly and slipped on his sunglasses. He couldn't help telling himself that the coming battle was going to be very interesting.

Sweetboy and Striker were thinking the same thing, but for different reasons. The hitman had been listening to the entire confrontation from his usual place on the office couch. He was looking forward to a fight worthy of him. Striker was still musing behind his desk, his fingers now wrapped together below his jaw.

"The Sunken Gardens at 8 o'clock." Sweetboy interrupted his thoughts. "I'll be there. And ready."

"No, you shall not," Striker said quietly, his clenched fists lightly tapping his chin. "You shall not even be near Brackenridge Park today."

Striker let it go at that, but Sweetboy wasn't about

to. For the first time in his tenure of employment, he got angry.

"What do you mean?" he demanded, rising off the couch. "I could understand all that other shit work you had me do, but this is my specialty. This is what I've been waiting for! You can't deny me this kill!"

Striker slowly dropped his hands to below the desktop level. Williams saw his neck and shoulder muscles tense minutely, as if Striker had just gripped something. The assassin decided that the businessman was either set to kill him or prepared to jack off.

"Inspector Callahan must die from a confrontation with duly authorized police officers. That is the only way he can die without arousing undue suspicion."

"Big deal!" Sweetboy pressed. "You can say my bullet was from a police gun! Christ! *He's* a cop and *he* uses a .44!"

"The meeting is at the park. In public. There may be witnesses."

"Innocent bystanders! They've been accidentally shot before."

"And you're just the man to shoot them," Striker reminded him sardonically. "The only blood that will be spilled will be Callahan's."

"Then get me a uniform! Hell, I'll get a uniform!"

"No. This death must be seamless. Reports must be made out."

Sweetboy stared at his boss. The businessman was sitting placidly behind his desk, both arms reaching underneath, his eyes half-closed. He was preparing himself for the kill, Williams realized. He's ready to mow me down on the spot.

With an effort, the hitman forced himself to relax. He shuddered, moved his head and shoulders around like a stiffened athlete, then sighed.

"All right," he said. "Yeah, I see your point."

Striker wanted to make sure. "Inspector Callahan will be regrettably killed this evening by the police force. They have their orders. He is a dangerous fugitive to be shot on sight. You, on the other hand, will be packing for a vacation. Have you ever been to Europe?"

"Sure," Williams answered, a chill moving down his arms. "I offed a guy in Paris once."

"Good. Then I'll be sending you to Britain. Or Ireland. Maybe the Alps. You'd like that, would you?"

"Sure."

"Good. Go home and pack. I'll send a car round for you at 8:00," Striker informed him purposely.

Without looking back and keeping up an innocent act, Sweetboy left the office.

Striker maintained just as convincing a facade. But he knew that Sweetboy was getting harder and harder to control. Maybe after the prolonged holiday, he'd get back to his pliable self.

Walking out of the businessman's mansion and crossing the beautifully maintained grounds to the huge garage, Sweetboy knew differently. He knew that if Striker knew about the Tucker house lie, he'd already be dead. And it was only a matter of time before the businessman found out. Sweetboy's time on the payroll was short. He'd pack for a long trip, all right, but he wouldn't be around his apartment when the car came to pick him up.

He had a date at 8:00. In Brackenridge Park.

The park was beautiful. It really was. Not only did it contain the Sunken Gardens and the Sunken Gardens Theater, it incorporated the Witte Museum of Fine Arts, the San Antonio Zoo, and the Old Trail Drivers Museum within its boundaries. It was a big place.

Even the Sunken Gardens alone was a big place. And it was a mastery of floral design. One great thing about floral design, Harry thought, is that it gave one plenty of cover. Besides the stone buildings designed in Oriental motifs, the gardens were packed with trees, shrubs, and bushes. Along with the flowers, they were illuminated by tall, thin, overhead lights.

Harry had picked the place perfectly. It afforded him a lot of room to breathe and to hide. One could wander around for minutes without being seen. The only real way to get a drop on anybody inside was to ride the overhead cable car, and even that was unreliable. If your quarry was inside one of the stone huts or firmly entrenched in a tree, the rock and leaf roofs would keep him out of sight.

After Harry had taken pains picking the place, he had taken pains planning the rendezvous. He had bought some food and brought it with him, so if Striker's men interviewed any area vendors they'd come up with nothing. Then he had made a thorough reconnaissance of the entire park. Only then did he slip into a phone booth and call Striker.

Reaching him had been no trouble. Keeping up a legitimate business front necessitated his company's name being in the phone book. And while one normally had to go through a barrage of secretaries and executives, the name Harry Callahan magically melted all the interference out of the way.

After he had hung up, Harry headed for the hiding places he had picked out. He spent the rest of the afternoon moving from one to another.

Finally dusk began to fall. The park lights went on. The crowds of tourists got sparser. The Sunken Gardens Theater's play started. The area all but emptied out. Two figures began to walk slowly down a darkened path.

Something about their walk attracted Harry's attention. The walk seemed practiced, patterned, almost unnatural. The two figures walked in a steady, identical manner. They walked like two seasoned policemen on foot patrol.

The figures came into the light. They weren't anybody Harry knew. They moved in a seemingly nonchalant manner, looking to and fro with exaggerated interest.

Harry smiled. They were cops, all right. Not only were they walking in unison, but they didn't know what to do with their hands. Take a uniformed patrolman's gun belt and nightstick away and you'll have one awkward dude.

Harry had two. This was the advance guard. Two relative innocents thrown into the shark's pool to see if he would bite. If these two made it through the Gardens without incident, Striker would probably start sending in the heavier guns.

Harry left the two sheep in plainclothes alone. He

needed to get a better idea of how Striker was going to handle the trade-off. So instead of tracking the uncomfortable plainclothesmen, he silently moved toward higher ground.

The Sunken Gardens were built in what was essentially a system of big holes. Harry had worked out a way of scaling the sides of the hole in ever increasing circles—hiding himself amidst flocks of sweet-smelling orchids. From time to time he felt like one of the Greek explorers getting lost among the lotuses. but the occasional dive-bombing bumblebee always brought him back to reality.

As soon as Harry settled in a bit higher up, some more obvious officers sidled into his sight-lines. These guys were a little more practiced than the first pair, but Harry knew cops when he saw them. As he watched, an even half-dozen fanned out toward all sides.

Striker wasn't taking chances. Harry reasoned. He had slipped through the businessman's fingers too many times for any love to be lost. This time Harry figured that Striker would choke the park with police.

Harry thought about surrendering. It wasn't something he often thought about. but for Carol Nash's sake, he was considering it. He had given Striker his word that he'd give himself up and, crooked or not, he wasn't about to start shooting cops to get back at the businessman. As long as Nash was brought to him alive and in one piece, he would go through with the exchange.

More cops stomped into the park. They entered the Gardens and spread out. The more that showed up, the less they seemed to care about looking inconspicuous. Some hardened vets even took up guard-like positions near the stone busildings.

Soon there was a veritable platoon below Harry. The inspector had little doubt that there was a platoon at each of the exits as well. Well, he couldn't blame them. His reputation and his actions in San Antonio added up to a very nasty collar. No cop wanted to tackle the likes of Callahan alone.

The stage was finally set. All the officers created a spotlight of flesh that concentrated Harry's attention on a single walkway. Harry shifted his position to get a better view of the pavement. He saw another two shadows at the other end. As he watched, the figures started moving toward the center of the Gardens.

Unlike the first pair, these two were handling themselves erratically. One seemed to be stumbling while the other seemed anxious, always moving ahead a couple of steps. When the illumination of an overhead lamp finally revealed them, Harry could understand why.

The stumbling man was Peter Nash. He had his hands cuffed in front of him and he looked like he had been cuffed by other hands. There were bruises all over his face. The anxious one turned out to be an even bigger surprise. First of all, his face looked worse than Nash's. He had a bandage completely covering his nose and a huge black and blue mark spread out from that across his face like rays from the sun. Pulling Nash along after him was Sheriff Strughold.

It was a bad sign. Harry had hoped the dupe was laid up in the hospital from his punch. If ol' Mitch was handling the trade, Harry's chance of reaching the jailhouse alive was slim. Before he could give himself up, he'd have to think of a way to ensure that he wouldn't be "regrettably killed while trying to escape."

If Harry could get into something else besides the sheriff's car, there was a good chance he could contact Bressler and the San Francisco boys before the roof fell in. Once that was accomplished he'd have to avoid the jailhouse knife-in-the-ribs or slit-throat or despondent-hanging-suicide ploy or any other mishap that's apt to befall a caged "enemy of the state."

To add to his problems, with Strughold shepherding Nash, there was no guarantee the ex-deputy would get back either. Harry could be safe in custody before Striker pulled the rug out from under all of them. In that case, Harry would have accomplished nothing.

Instead of making a decision, Harry counted the cops in his immediate vicinity. There were two near the doorway of the stone building. There were four lounging near the middle of the walkway. There were two more near Strughold and Nash. There were three others keeping their eyes on various flower arrangements. Just under a dozen men against one man and a helpless, handcuffed hostage.

Almost of its own volition, the .44 Magnum was out and in his hand. He crouched in the flowers, ready to move off to the right and get behind Strughold and his prisoner. So he was ready when the first explosion came.

A crackling boom suddenly echoed across the Gardens. Harry looked down at his own gun in surprise, then saw a flash in his peripheral vision. He jerked his head up in time to see the second cop behind Strughold crumble to the ground. The first cop had already fallen, his gun barrel still smoking.

Bursting out from the shadows was a big, muscular man with a huge silenced Magnum revolver. For the first time, Harry laid eyes on Sweetboy Williams.

He must've been in 'Nam, was the first thing Harry thought because the hitman was wearing a completely black outfit and his face was smeared with grease. He had blended in with the night perfectly. And nobody could use a Magnum that well and that fast without some sort of concerted practice. The only real place for concerted practice was either in police academies or the military and Sweetboy sure as hell wasn't no ex-cop! Not the way he mowed down the officers present without a shred of remorse or hesitation.

Harry saw the assassin's left arm swing at Strughold while his right hand aimed the silenced Magnum. He hit the sheriff and killed the cops at the building entrance at the same time. All three crumbled. Williams in action was astonishing.

The remaining cops' first thought was not to avenge their fallen comrades; it was not to join them. The others scrambled behind any cover they could find as Sweetboy grabbed Nash around the neck. Harry broke out from his cover as the hitman dragged the ex-deputy back the way he had come.

Callahan raced across the flowers, trampling beautiful buds as he went. He leaped onto the sidewalk just in time to see Sweetboy cut across the theater grounds and for the hiding cops to show themselves again. To them, one big silhouette with a Magnum was just like any other, so they started firing on Harry.

The sidewalk ripped apart with little asphalt gushers as Harry went after Williams. The theater was built on the edge of the river which wound its way through the entire park. There was a bridge connecting an open-air summer theater stage with a bleacher section of seats on the other side. Williams and Nash were dodging in and out of the bleachers as Harry stepped out onto the stage.

The only applause he got was in the form of .44-caliber bullets. Williams may have been good, but no one was good enough to hit Harry with anything from across a river in the middle of the evening. Harry leveled his own weapon and snapped off a shot.

It was a mistake. Not only had he jeopardized Nash's continual breathing but he set up a booming beacon for the other cops to follow. Harry didn't want them to catch him midway across the bridge, so he ran to the stage edge and dropped into the water.

That wasn't a mistake. Not only didn't the arriving policeman spot him, but he was able to follow Williams by simply floating down the shallow river.

The Paseo was so shallow at that point that Harry was able to crouch beneath the walled-up bank with his torso and weapon out of the H_2O. He listened as the cops scanned the opposite bank for any sign of their prey. He heard them admit defeat and plan to spread out and search. Harry grinned. Both he and Sweetboy had gotten away from the cops again, but Sweetboy hadn't gotten away from him. Not yet he hadn't. Harry pushed off down the river.

He pulled himself out of the drink in front of a wooded area into which he saw two shadowy figures disappear. The night had taken on a quietly ominous atmosphere. The bright lights of the park only added to the feeling by cutting through the treetops like laser beams. It was a night of blue shadows and pale white bolts. The evening's warmth started coming off the water in the form of mist. Harry rose from the river like a gun-toting Creature from the Black Lagoon.

He dripped across the woods, remembering the last two times he had done the same. In Los Angeles he had wound up in the middle of a Western movie. This time he was close. He wound up facing the entrance to the Old Trail Drivers Museum. The front door, which should have been locked, was wavering in the night wind. It shuddered open for a moment, then clacked close, only to blow slightly open again.

Harry walked over and went inside without pausing. As soon as he was in he moved quickly to the other side of the entrance. He waited on his haunches for his eyes to become accustomed to the dark. About thirty seconds later, just as it seemed they had, the lights went on.

But only for a second. Long enough for Harry to see Sweetboy seeing him. He saw the hitman's gun point at him, then the lights went off again.

He heard the cough of Williams' gun and the tinkle of broken glass even as he was diving toward the open door. As he slapped the unlocked entry open and rolled away he heard a slapping sound on the floor where he had been.

He righted himself as the door banged against the wall and bounced closed again, allowing the dim moonlight into the museum in an ever widening then ever thinning band. That weak illumination was enough to let Harry glimpse Sweetboy moving deeper into the museum. Strangely, Nash was nowhere to be seen.

Remembering the exhibits' placements from the splitsecond the lights were on, Harry followed Sweetboy's lead. He moved carefully, his gun held out of harm's way, one arm out and his feet silently shuffling across the floor. As soon as he had attained the second room, the lights went on again.

Sweetboy was aiming at him from over the driver's seat of an old-fashioned flatbed wagon. He fired and the bullet splattered into the wall next to Harry's head. Harry fired back, his bullet biting off a hunk of the wooden handbrake next to Sweetboy's cranium. The lights went off again.

Harry ran forward, hoping to cut Sweetboy off

where he saw him last. When he reached the flatbed in the darkness, he heard footsteps moving in the opposite direction. The lights went on again. Sweetboy was leaning out the back of a covered wagon, gun swinging in Harry's direction.

Callahan shot first this time, right through the cloth of the wagon. The bullet billowed the material from both sides but streaked over Sweetboy's right shoulder. His silenced pistol leveled in his left hand, the hitman fired back, ripping off an entire plank from the side of the flatbed.

Harry ran until he was looking through the covered wagon from the front. Sweetboy was jumping out the back. Harry fired again, neatly cutting off a lock of Williams' hopping hair. Sweetboy landed, bent to his knees and shot under the wagon. His bullet went between Harry's legs. The lights went off again.

The light show was driving Harry's pupils crazy. He had to get into a room that had a little consistent illumination. He didn't worry about Sweetboy. Where Harry went, the hitman would follow. Lord knows Callahan had followed him long enough—it was about time he returned the favor.

Harry stayed quiet and still until he thought he sensed some blue amid the blackness. A strange thing about darkness; it had a way of throwing off all one's other senses as well. All Harry had to go on was instinct and common sense. All the rooms couldn't be windowless and all the windows couldn't be covered, so it was just a matter of finding that room. Keeping a pair of mental fingers crossed, Harry followed the feeling of blue.

A few steps later and he was feeling a bit more secure. The blue was getting stronger. A few more feet and he was certain. He was following a definite light to its source. The trail led into another room. There Harry could see a line of bright beige, like the semblance of a lamp escaping through the crack of a door. Harry marched up to it and put his hand up where a doorknob should be.

A round globe of metal slipped into his hand. He twisted, pulled, and pushed his gun inside the tiny room.

The rest of the area was immediately bathed in illumination, revealing the last room in the museum. It was a storage area in the back, complete with an emergency exit door and the control closet, into which Harry was presently pointing his revolver. At that moment, the lights went on again.

Right in front of his barrel was a blinking Peter Nash. His hands were still cuffed in front of him, but all his fingers were poised over the switches that controlled the spolights for the entire museum. The ex-deputy's eyes were glazed and half-closed. It was obvious he hadn't recognized Harry yet. But before the inspector could say anything, both the back door and entrance door flew open.

Cops started pouring in through the back and Sweetboy appeared framed in the front.

"Kill the lights!" the hitman screamed.

It was Harry who complied. Nash froze up in confusion, so Callahan shifted his aim to zero in on the light box. Nash fell back as Harry pulled the trigger. There was an explosion of sparks, and then the entire museum was bathed in blue again.

It was a blue that was soon filled with yellow-orange specks. The cops blasted away with careless abandon. To their way of thinking, they had nothing to worry about. As far as they were concerned, all their targets were mad-dog killers. It was every bullet for itself.

Harry hit the floor and crawled deeper into the control booth, hoping to make contact with Nash's legs. Although he found himself against the rear wall, the ex-deputy had seemed to disappear magically. Harry sat up and listened. Among the hectic police gunshots, he could hear a rapid coughing and the noise four feet made when running. According to all evidence, Sweetboy was making good his getaway still in Nash's company.

Even though he hated the hitman's guts, Harry found a lot to admire about him. He could appreciate Sweetboy's ability, speed, and accuracy. Given all that to commend him, Harry thought it best to follow the assassin's example. When the smoke cleared and the lights went back on, he didn't want to be around with any dead cops riddled with .44 Magnum holes.

Harry waited until all the cops stampeded through the back room and into the museum. Then he went out the back door. The river floated him to safety beyond the park cordon.

Eight

"Again? You let him get away again?" Hannibal Striker was incredulous. Mitch Strughold was in pain.

"For Christsake, Sweetboy showed up! He hit me and started going crazy!"

"I know that!" Striker raged. "I can believe that! What I can't believe is that you let Williams, Nash, and Callahan get away from you again!"

The businessman rose from behind his desk and paced across the thick white carpet. Never before had he been so amazed at one man's performance. For years his empire had run well and his power had seemed absolute. Then one lousy inspector from Los Angeles shows up and the whole thing falls apart. His own personal hitman turns into an obsessive cowboy, desperate for a gunfight at the OK Corral, and his own personal lawman turns into an incompetent, accident-prone idiot.

"We'll find him," said Strughold in pleading tones from the couch. "There are only so many places Callahan can go . . . !"

"Callahan!" Striker roared again, the veins on his

neck getting as big as shotgun barrels. "Who gives a fuck about Callahan?"

"But I thought . . ." the sheriff stuttered.

"Don't think!" Striker commanded. "Do! Find Sweetboy Williams and kill him!"

"But what about Nash's evidence?" Strughold asked, confused. "If he knew all about the payoffs, he must have a hell of a lot of evidence somewhere."

"It's hidden," the businessman said very quietly, putting his arms on either side of the sheriff's shoulders, which rested on the back of the couch. "Nash wouldn't tell us where it is and we couldn't find it so that means that no one else is likely to find it either.

"But," Striker continued, his voice rising in volume, "Williams knows enough about this operation to bury me, you, and everybody else in the city! And if he decides to do any harmonizing with Nash, it'll kill every crooked official in the state! Forget about Nash's papers. We could tear his whole house apart and not find them. Find Williams! Kill Williams!"

The sheriff had been right for once. There were only a few places Harry could go. He had already used Tucker's place. He could hole up on public property, but that was a losing proposition. He needed time to think, plan, and eat. Another change of clothes wouldn't hurt either.

It was the latter desire that made up Callahan's mind. Taking plenty of time to stake out the grounds, Harry slipped into Nash's neighborhood, waited until night, then broke into the ex-deputy's cellar. He stumbled over to the stairs, flicked on the light, and looked right down the barrel of a service revolver.

Lucky for him, Carol Nash was holding it. She took one look at her target, dropped the gun like it had suddenly heated up to five hundred degrees, and fell sobbing into Harry's arms.

After Harry changed into his original pair of pants that Carol had washed so long ago, eaten, and cleaned up, he started tearing the basement apart.

"What are you looking for?" Carol asked from her seat on the cellar steps.

"I'm not sure," said Harry. "Some papers. A file. A book. I don't know, just something that could tell me a little more about what I'm fighting against."

Carol picked at the stitching of her designer jeans. "Harry," she began tentatively. "Is it all worth it? I mean, all the planning. All the games. Boris' death. Your coming here . . . ." She let her spoken thought trail off.

Harry turned from the mess he was making of the wall. "What are you asking?"

"I mean . . . do you think . . . is Peter all right?"

Harry thought about soothing her. He thought about being optimistic. But there was something in Carol's voice that told him to be truthful. "I don't know." Then there was something in his own mind that told him to add, "I doubt it."

Carol nodded and looked down at the section of jean she was picking. Harry went back to the wall, irritated. He had to admit it to himself. Carol had hit the nail right on the head. It had been a gigantic game to Nash. All the research, all the arrests, all the work was just expended so he could realize a pet theory of law enforcement. All the give and take didn't have any reality for him. He was happy to sit in his cellar and do all the planning while Tucker had had to walk into the fire.

Only the fire had come looking for Deputy Nash. He was a pawn in a larger game of hide and seek. And Harry really couldn't bring himself to feel sorry for him. Nash had been playing with matches thinking he'd never get burned. He had all the righteous smugness of a general who sent his men into battle. It wouldn't keep Harry from doing everything he could to save him, but it kept him from feeling any sort of pity.

"I guess I wasn't a very good cop's wife," came Carol's voice into his thoughts. Harry looked to find the woman had moved over to stand right beside him. "I'd have lunch with all the other men's wives and they'd all be talking about what their husbands did," she continued, "and I'd think about Peter working away in here. I remember him planning a particularly big arrest. He was using..." she moved her hand around in the air, "... little chess pieces. That's all the others were to him. And that was all right... for a while. I felt the police needed him. They needed a planner." She looked up at Harry's face almost apologetically. "Peter didn't like to get his hands dirty."

"What changed your mind?" Harry asked quietly.

Carol placed her hands on the wall and lowered her head until it was resting between her palms. "I met Sheriff Tucker... Boris. He wasn't a piece of plastic. He was... so alive."

Harry remembered the man Carol was trying to describe. She was right. Tucker was one of those men who lived what all those actors faked in beer commercials. More than anyone else Harry knew, Tucker lived with gusto. He didn't have to sail boats, or work on an oil rig, or break broncos to really live. Tucker was a man who improved the world by just being in it. The way his wife loved him and the way his kids were growing up proved that.

"I—I started to see something in Peter I had never seen before. As he planned out all these dangerous things for real people to do..." She stopped, embarrassed by her awkward confessions. "You know," she added suddenly, "I could never call him Pete?" She laughed at that, a high, barking laugh that died as soon as it was born. "He just wasn't the 'Pete' kind," she finished sadly.

Harry took her into his arms as the tears began to roll down her cheeks.

"Oh God, Harry," she choked out between short sobs. "I feel—I feel..."

She never finished her thought. And whatever it was, it didn't keep them from making love.

Later on, if Harry ever was feeling a little bit cynical, a little bit loose, and a little philosophical with his barroom buddies, he might have called what he had with Carol Nash as sex of the very best kind. It was a slightly illicit emotion combined with shared fear, need, and desire. It was dangerous because of the threat all around them; dirty, because she was another man's wife; and desperate, because they both felt it might be the last love they'd ever experience.

That might be how Harry would term it if he ever talked about it. But Harry would never talk about it. And Harry wasn't analyzing it. And Harry wasn't enjoying it. It went beyond anything like that. It was like the rest of his life. He was doing it because he thought it was right and he had to.

He awoke with his conscience speaking. It was a small police voice in his head telling him the woes of the world. At first he thought it was a dream. But then his eyes snapped open and his brain completely cleared. There was a tiny police voice speaking, and it was coming from somewhere up above.

Carol shifted in her sleep and mumbled something against his chest. He looked down at her sleeping face framed by a cascade of dark hair. It was a shame that she looked so good, Harry thought. He might feel less guilt if she were a dog.

He gingerly slipped his arm out from under her and got out of bed. Her weight had cut off all blood in the limb, so Harry moved outside with what felt like a log attached to his shoulder. He moved around the house's upper story until he pinpointed the sound as coming from an attic opening in the ceiling.

There was a string hanging down from the opening which Harry pulled to reveal a folded ladder. Stretching it out, he hopped up the rungs until his head poked up into the warm dark room made by the house's roof. The voice grew louder.

Something brushed against his forehead. He jerked back thinking it was a bug of some kind. But then he saw another string hovering before him. He grabbed it and pulled. There was a click and then there was light.

The voice was coming from an impressive ham radio outfit in the corner of the attic. Harry moved all the way up and walked over to the chair in front of the large, sit-down machine. The entire thing came up to Harry's stomach and was almost three times as wide. The sloping face of the radio was covered in switches and dials and had one long microphone on an adjustable arm smack-dab in the middle.

A green felt-covered desk came off of that, covered with schedules, notes, and an incongruous-looking, long-barrelled .22 revolver. Beneath that, between the radio's thick legs, were mounds of multicolored wire that seemed to grow right into the wall.

"Peter's computer," said Carol Nash, taking Harry by surprise. He turned to see her at the top of the attic ladder, wearing a peach-colored nightgown and hugging herself with wrapped arms. "Between the cellar and the attic I never saw him."

Harry turned his attention back to the radio, trying to find some way to control it. "A regular Batman, wasn't he?" he commented.

"Had it on an automatic timer," Carol explained, coming over. "It would always go on at the damndest times. I—I guess I forgot to unplug it." Harry kept checking it out, so the woman thought it necessary to keep explaining. "He gathered a lot of his intelligence from that. Collected it all and entered it into that thing over there."

Harry looked toward where she was pointing. A tiny Apple home computer sat in a corner next to a small Sony black and white television set. Next to those was a tape-carrying case.

The brainstorm came when he was looking at the case. Ignoring the radio for the moment, Harry got up slowly and moved like a mesmerized man toward the computer. Carol watched his progress with a questioning expression. Harry moved past the TV and the keyboard to the case. It wasn't locked. He flipped it open to reveal twenty-four cassette tapes; eight in three columns.

Neatly typed onto the cassette spines were the names of different video games. In the first column there were such things as "Blackjack," "Space Attack," "Backgammon," and "Lunar Landing." Harry riffed through them all, not finding what he wanted at first glance. Carol came over to look over his shoulder.

"Oh, the kids loved that one," she commented,

pointing at the tape marked "Superman." "A little computer man with a cape catches falling planes."

That gave Harry his second brainstorm of the night. "Was there any game he didn't let the kids play?"

"Yes," Carol said musingly. "One. He said it was too complicated for them." She pointed.

Harry should have known. It was the cassette marked "Cops and Robbers."

It wound up being too complicated for the San Francisco inspector as well. After fifteen minutes of concentrated effort, Harry was unable to get the cassette to give up its program on the video screen of the TV set. He tried several other tapes to make sure it was the taped computer "program" that wasn't working right and not him.

He turned on the set, which had no channel selector. He pushed the power button on the computer console. He stuck the "Space Battle" cassette into the tape recorder attached to the TV. The TV screen flashed "ready." Harry pressed the "Entry" button on the keyboard. Sure enough, a fleet of UFOs appeared among a set of video cross-hairs.

The computer was working, but the "Cops and Robbers" cassette didn't seem to. That made sense, Harry figured. Nash wouldn't have wanted just anyone to decipher his evidence. Harry tried a series of possible codes. After installing the cassette and the screen flashed "Ready," he typed in "TUCKER," and pressed "entry." Nothing.

He tried "PETER NASH," "CAROL," "STRIKER," and "VILLAVEDA." Still nothing. Then it occurred to him that Nash may have changed the code regularly for an extra measure of safety. He thought about Nash's reasoning. What would Nash have used to win a "Cops and Robbers" game?

Harry typed his own name and pressed entry. Again nothing. He grinned. That's what he got for harboring delusions of grandeur. Nash probably didn't think he was the answer. But, not to leave any base unchecked, he typed in "DIRTY HARRY." He pressed entry. For the last time, nothing. Harry was about to give up when he

135

thought about what was really destroying Striker's system.

He typed in ".44 MAGNUM." He pressed the entry button. Facts started spilling across the TV screen.

Harry spent another fifteen minutes taking in the incredible labyrinth of facts that Nash had compiled. There was enough in just that amount to put Striker and most of the Sheriff's office away for several lifetimes. If all of Nash's facts were verifiable, the businessman would come up for parole in 2250.

Harry stopped the tape, rewound it, ejected it, put it back into its plastic holder, and carried it downstairs. He turned the home computer off but left the ham radio on. Carol had lost interest ten minutes before, so as Harry dressed, he smelled the welcome aroma of bacon and eggs from the kitchen.

Carol Nash had washed his shirt to boot, so Harry put on the soft shirt, slipped into his own pants, Boris Tucker's boots, and Fred Tucker's corduroy jacket. For the first time since coming to San Antonio, he was feeling a little good. With his Magnum in its holster and the cassette tape in his pocket, he saw a little light down at the end of the Tucker case. All he had to do was deliver the evidence to the proper authorities.

Unfortunately, he didn't know who the proper authorities were. There was no way of being sure of any Texas cop with Striker's money reigning supreme, so it became a matter of getting out of the state. That is, getting out of the state after settling the score somewhat.

He went down to breakfast smiling, secure in the knowledge that revenge in this case was practical. First, it would be mighty hard for him to get over state lines the way things were. He'd have to clear his name a bit so that every ranger wouldn't be hot for his blood. Second, by the time he got back to Frisco and processed the evidence, both Striker and Sweetboy would probably be long gone. Harry had to settle accounts then and there.

Strangely, with Carol still in her nightgown and three eggs with six pieces of bacon waiting for him, the only thing Harry really noticed in the kitchen was another radio, this one being a short-wave jobbie that picked up police calls. Harry sat down at the small Formica table and dug into the grub while keeping his ears open.

The radio reports were interrupted by Carol Nash. She sat down across from him, poked at her food, then put her chin in a cupped hand and sighed.

"So what do I do now?" she wanted to know.

"What do you mean?" Harry asked around a hunk of egg.

"I washed your shirt, cooked you breakfast, and cleaned the basement. I had already sent the kids to their grandmother and checked out our savings. So what do I do now?"

Harry leaned back and pushed himself away from the table. "You're acting like Peter Nash is already dead."

"He is," she said indifferently, "to me."

"He may need you very badly after this," he reminded her.

"He never needed me," she answered, staring at her mushed-up eggs. "I was an obligation he promised himself. Aw, who knows where he is now. I've never known." She looked to Harry for some sort of affirmation. She saw that Harry was not looking at her. His gaze was intent on the police band radio and one hand was held up in a "silence" sign.

All she heard was a set of jumbled numbers and something about a call for "extra officers." Harry took it as a clarion call to duty. He wiped his mouth with his hand and stood. He tapped the jacket pockets, then he pulled open the jacket and pulled out his revolver. He broke it open, snapped it shut, spun the chamber, and stuck it snugly back into the shoulder holster.

"Can I use your car?" he asked Carol offhandedly.

"Keys are over in that dish by the back door," Carol replied automatically, feeling like she and Harry were an old married couple or brother and sister or father and daughter or something unquestionable like that. "Harry, what is it?"

"I think they've cornered Sweetboy," he said, picking up the keys. "And where Sweetboy is, your husband probably is, too."

Carol rose from the table and moved to Harry's side. "What are you going to do?" she asked, feeling foolish.

Harry shrugged. They stared at each other for what seemed like a minute. Harry was waiting for her to say anything she might need to. She couldn't think of anything. Instead she frowned for a second, looked back at the kitchen, then squeezed Harry's upper arm. Harry leaned down and kissed her quickly. She smiled. Bravely. Self-consciously. He opened the door to go.

"Harry," she called.

He stopped and turned.

"I'll be here if he needs me," she assured him.

"OK," Harry said and left. He never saw Carol Nash again.

As Jack Webb might put it, San Antonio is a big town. The major center lies in a neat oblong shape near the center of Texas. Just to the east of the central city is a suburban center nicely nestled among cypress, oak, and pecan trees. To the east of that is a thin line of railroad tracks, cars, and stations. Directly to the east of that is the sprawling Golden State Beer Brewery.

Like the drunk at the Four Ponies had said, everything's big in Texas, and the brewery was no exception. First there was a series of wooded glens, neatly sculptured. After that was a system of lakes, perfect for recreation. Then there was the brewery proper; an interconnected series of buildings that ranged from public exhibits to a public restaurant to the actual beer-making facilities. Beyond that were the truck loading platforms and a huge parking lot. All together, the establishment stretched over fifty acres.

So if it was so big, why can't I find it, Harry asked himself. He had gotten on Route 81, but kept on winding up in Windcrest County. The only good thing about getting lost, Harry figured, was that he could catch up on the scuttlebutt coming from any one of Nash's car's three radios.

From yet another portable police band system Harry found out the police were waiting for a meeting with the brewery owner and the sheriff's office before moving in. From the installed CB, Harry heard about the hitman. According to regular newscasts, the man inside the brewery was just another gun-toting nut with a hostage and a mad-on. According to the truckers he was a cornered mad-dog killer harboring a grudge. Harry didn't know how these good ol' boys on eight wheels always seemed to know these things, but he blessed their macho little hearts.

And he blessed the heart of K-NEW, San Antonio's all-news AM radio station. One particularly intrepid reporter had tracked down the brewery's owner for a hasty talk. Although the owner was non-committal, surly, and uncooperative, his very existence brought the whole brewery siege into focus. The owner of Golden State Beer's San Antonio Brewery was Hannibal Striker. H. A. to his friends.

Harry got off the Route 410 loop and headed downtown. He was just in time for the end of the strategy meeting at the sheriff's office.

Striker and Strughold headed for the sheriff's car, instructing Mitch's two deputies to follow in another. Both men watched the young cops get into another patrol car as they slid into the front seat of their own. Strughold took the driver's seat, despite the bandages on his nose and the large Band-Aid on his head. The sheriff turned the key, the engine roared into life, and the car lurched forward.

It wasn't until they were well on their way to the brewery on Highway 90 that anyone spoke.

"It went all right. I suppose," said the sheriff.

"Of course," snapped Striker. "We couldn't let the regular force move in and take him. It has to be you and your men And you cannot, under any circumstances, bring him out alive."

"But it's a big place," Strughold complained, "and Sweetboy knows it like the back of his hand. I don't relish goin' in thar with jest two of my men."

"Then I'll make you a deal," said Harry Callahan

from the back seat, sitting up from the floor and sticking the barrel of his Magnum against Striker's neck.

"Callahan!" the businessman boomed in surprise.

"I do get around, don't I?" Harry said, smiling.

"Yer crazy!" the sheriff yelled, trying to drive, stare at the inspector, and think of a way out at the same time. "When we get to the brewery you'll be wrapped in more chains than a whore into leather!"

"Who says we'll get to the brewery?" Harry inquired innocently. "A small accident. A fiery wreck. Two of San Antonio's finest citizens killed. They might never find the bullet holes in your charred bodies."

"What do you want?" Striker demanded.

"A truce," Harry said immediately. "You pull in your long arm for a minute and let me go after Sweetboy."

"Yer crazy!" the Sheriff said again.

"Shut up," hissed Striker. "What's the deal?" he asked Harry, his voice low.

"Same as before," Harry answered. "Me and my crimes for Nash's life."

Striker turned in his seat to look over the Magnum barrel. He was smiling. "You *are* crazy."

Harry leaned back in the rear seat, keeping his gun pointed at the businessman. "We've been through that before," he said wearily. "We have a deal?"

"We have a deal," Striker agreed. Strughold kept silent, but Harry didn't miss the look they gave one another. It was the look of two inventors of a better mouse trap chauffeuring a test rat to their lab.

Harry mentally shrugged. He *was* crazy, but this was the only way he saw of getting inside the brewery without his hide being perforated. But he had little doubt that the sheriff was saving that for last. Striker was probably already thinking of more ways he could turn Harry into Swiss cheese.

Strughold got to the brewery with no trouble. The parking lot was filled with police cars; all their turrets flashing and whirling. The sheriff pulled right up to the factory's entrance and got out, his hands held up in the face of a dozen reporters and police officials running up to meet him.

Harry put his gun away and got out the other side. He held the door open for Striker. A police lieutenant looked from Harry to Strughold with a strange expression, but the Sheriff smiled and nodded.

"It's all right, Ted," he told the policeman. "He's in custody."

Ted looked at Harry again. Callahan shrugged as if saying "what're ya gonna do?" He then glanced at Striker's stone face and moved around the front of the car to join Strughold. The sheriff's deputies drove up, saw what was happening, brought the car to a screeching halt and leaped out of the vehicle with their guns drawn.

"That's all right, that's all right," the sheriff soothed the quizzical newsmen and the aiming deputies. "This is Inspector Callahan from San Francisco, folks. We have reason to believe he might be implemental in capturing the alleged perpetrator inside."

"Instrumental," Harry corrected.

"Thank you, Inspector Callahan," Strughold said laboriously. "Come on, come on, boys," the sheriff spat at his deputies, still holding their guns on Harry. "Now put yer weapons away and c'mon!"

The sheriff led the way to the front door of the brewery. Harry waited until the deputies holstered their guns and followed, casting back furtive glances at him. He brought up the rear. Strughold held the door open for his men. Harry took it out of his hands and motioned "after you." The Sheriff scowled and went in.

Before he entered Harry heard the beginning of a joint statement to the press by Striker and the police chief. The chief assured the public that he would not allow any terrorist to hold them captive and commended Striker on his firm action. Striker thanked his "old and dear friend," then went on to repeat that they were not sure as to the identity of either the gunman or his hostage.

Harry snorted and went inside. The difference between the brewery's exterior and interior was stunning.

Outside, it was a squat, greyish building. Inside it was cool, burnished wood, and luxurious. The entrance was a wide hallway with murals painted on either wall, cross-beams on the roof and stained wooden columns down the middle of the solid maroon flooring.

The three cops walked ahead of Harry, seemingly oblivious of his company. They were covering all the bases, Harry realized. Since Striker had said that they didn't know who the gunman and his hostage were, the sheriff couldn't be blamed for gunning them both down. And if the visiting Frisco inspector just happened to be caught in the cross fire, then that was just too bad.

The only thing Harry felt sure of was that they weren't going to turn their guns on him until they had moved a little deeper into the brewery. They couldn't have the press finding Harry's corpse before the hitman and his hostage were even located, now could they? Only thing was that Harry wasn't going to give them a chance to catch him unawares.

He slowed his pace until the trio of cops was almost half a hallway down from him. They were heading for the doors at the other end. The doors that led to the exhibits and then the brewery. Harry spied a door to his right. Keeping an eye on the cops' backs, he turned silently and pushed through it.

He got into the new room with no trouble. The door hadn't been locked and the sheriff hadn't noticed his detour. By the looks of the small office, Harry had walked into the manager's or night watchman's room. Across a desk that filled most of the office was a large window. There was no visible latch or other means of opening it so Harry picked up a chair and hurled it through the glass. That brought the deputies running.

But as soon as they had heard the window shatter, Harry was up onto the desk and leaping through the opening. By the time the trio of cops burst into the room, Harry was halfway across the adjoining courtyard, racing toward a roofed patio that stretched all the way around the area.

The sheriff wasn't going to stand on ceremony. He shoved his associates out of the way and started shooting.

Harry made it across the patio and into another door across the way as the bullets ineffectively slapped into nearby trees and grassy mounds.

One of the deputies started to crawl out of the window after him, but the sheriff pulled him roughly back. "All the halls lead to the brewery," he said. "We'll run into him again soon enough."

Harry was thinking the same thing the sheriff was saying. He knew the time of reckoning was at hand, but he wanted to fight it on his own terms. What he didn't want was three crooked cops letting him have it when he wasn't looking.

The inspector ran through a gallery of different wild-life dioramas. As he moved down each hall and turned each corner deeper and deeper in the brewery, more and more types of animals stared at him from trophies on the wall, stands on the floor, and glass-encased boxes serving double-duty as windows. As he passed all these frozen, lifeless examples of nature he heard a grinding hum getting louder and louder. He was nearing the actual brewery section.

The Golden State Brewery was one establishment that did it all. It soaked the barley and heated it into malt before grinding it. It mixed the malt with water while adding the necessary cereals. That mixture, called wort, was then heated again, stirred, and filtered. Hops and yeast were added before fermentation in huge metallic vats. The process went on seven days a week, twenty-four hours a day. Only now the staff had been emptied out because Sweetboy showed up.

The hitman had chosen his Waterloo well. It being Striker's establishment, Sweetboy probably felt secure that Strughold would be coming after him. And with Strughold showing up, he probably figured Harry wouldn't be far behind. He was right, Harry admitted to himself. It was an educated guess all the way around. Even if he hadn't stumbled on Sweetboy's hideout from following the sheriff or listening to the radio, the assassin probably could've made good his escape after getting rid of Nash's dead weight.

The buzz of the brewery was getting louder. Harry

slowed down. He didn't want to speed around a corner right into the waiting weapons of the sheriff or Sweetboy. Harry started stalking purposefully across the brown tiles. He had twenty-one rounds left. He had checked his ammo after cleaning his wet gun a second time at Nash's house. He had three rounds left over from the fight at Brackenridge Park and three auto-loaders beyond that. That left about five bullets for each of his possible targets, with one for good luck.

Harry had come to the end of the exhibits. He passed a circular portrait of all the Golden State beverage products. Beautifully rendered were cans and bottles of their regular brew, their draft beer, their light beer, and their ale. Just next to that was a double swing doorway with the words "No Entry Beyond This Point" written across it. Above the doorway were several Golden State Beer signs emblazoned with their mottos: "A Brew As Big As Texas!" and "Double Brewed, Double Delicious!"

There were no windows on the doors but the hum was heavy behind it. Harry pulled out the Magnum, set himself, and burst through.

As soon as the doors burst open, the gunshots started. Bullets smashed between Harry's feet and into the door as he fell and rolled toward cover. Out of the corner of his eye he had spied a sign-in desk. Harry rolled to that as a temporary cover.

He looked up to see one of Strughold's deputies on a catwalk between two vats above him. The cop tried to hit Harry with another shot. Harry ducked beneath the desk lip again. The bullet plowed into the desk top. If the deputy had shot nearer the desk edge, his .357 bullet might have gotten through the wood and into Harry's back.

As it was, the deputy pulled his gun up and ran. Harry took the moment to take aim. At the last possible second before the deputy made it to safety, Harry eased up on the trigger. It wouldn't do to waste a bullet just to let the creep know he was there. He'd save his lead for a sure thing.

Standing up, Harry took in the entire area with a quick glance. After the sign-in desk came a row of six vats. Above them were a system of catwalks crisscrossing another system of conveyer belts. These two systems moved downward behind the vats to end at a group of tall, rectangular storing structures. Beyond those were three metal stairwells; one on the right wall, one on the left, and one in the center of the back wall. At each level, the stairs were connected by long landings that stretched from one wall to the other.

Just to make the examination complete, Harry glanced over his shoulder. There were two stairways behind him that led to the catwalks. He raced up the nearest one as the sounds of gunfire echoed from the other side of the big room.

Harry had made it to the second level when a bullet splattered against the wall high over his head. He looked up and over the landing to see the second deputy firing madly back the way he had run. That told Harry that Sweetboy was at the other end of the enclosure, making a stand on the far third level. The only question left for Callahan to answer was where were Nash and Strughold?

By the time Harry set foot on the third level, he was too busy to consider any possible answers. The first deputy was waiting for him. He was crouching against the top of a vat on the right side aiming at Harry while his partner was behind a vat on the left side firing at Sweetboy. The only thing between Harry and the deputies were another two vats. The inspector imagined the same would be true for Sweetboy.

Harry dodged, pivoted, and leaped behind the top of the closest vat as the first deputy opened fire again. As he dropped behind the shiny silver structure, he heard a pop and felt something cold and wet splash across his head. He looked up into a beer shower. Ignoring the frosty liquid, Harry fell to his stomach on the left of the vat, crawled around to the other side and squeezed off a shot at the first deputy who was still waiting for him to appear on the right side.

The .44 bullet punched into the other vat right next to the first deputy's ear. Instead of blood, golden liquid shot out, then continued pouring in a steady stream. Harry noticed that the fight between the hitman and the second deputy had already made the catwalk slick with beer. The stuff was foaming over the sides and onto the floor below.

Even though Harry had shot dangerously close to the first deputy, the crooked cop couldn't take cover on the other side or he'd be right in Sweetboy's sights. The only chance the deputies had was to keep their targets so busy that they didn't have time to pick the vulnerable lawmen off.

The first deputy did just that. His only reaction to Harry's first shot was to jerk his head out of the way, squint his eyes, and fire three shots back. Harry jumped back under cover just as the third of those bullets whacked into the vat. If the metal hadn't been in the way, Harry would have made a home for the lead in his side.

Rather than roll to the other side of the vat and fire from there, Harry stretched around the corner he had just come from and prepared to shoot the first deputy. According to his bullet count, the deputy would have two bullets left to Harry's five. The odds were right but the first deputy wasn't there. Harry was stunned for a second, but it was almost a second too long.

He whirled just in time to crumble away from the first deputy racing around the right corner of the vat. Instead of holding tight, the cop had charged. Harry crumbled quickly because the deputy was firing as he came around the corner. The second to last bullet whipped over Harry's head. The last bullet creased Harry's ear.

Harry raised his Magnum and fired. The booming bullet grabbed the running deputy by the chest and pushed. The already-dead cop's feet and arms flew forward while his torso leaped back. He slammed against a vat fully five feet away and crumbled to the catwalk, a little river of beer coursing around him.

Harry hopped to his feet and charged around the corner to peg the second deputy. As soon as he broke cover, he cursed himself for being a little too eager. Sweetboy was no longer pinning the second cop down. The second cop was ready and willing to face Harry.

The two stood in the open and exchanged a flurry of rapid fire. Each man would shoot, dodge, and shoot again. For two full seconds the twenty foot area between them was filled with ricocheting sparks, whining lead and newly made faucets of beer.

Harry had two bullets left in the chamber and no time to reload. He stood his ground. The deputy fired again. Harry felt a heat whiz by his ribs. Harry fired. The cop ducked at that exact moment. Another fountain of beer coursed out above the crouching deputy. The deputy pulled his trigger. His hammer clicked on an empty chamber.

Harry wrapped his other hand around the Magnum butt, started squeezing the trigger, put a foot forward to steady himself, and slipped.

The flowing brew had laid a trap for him. It had all but hydroplaned his shoe, and there was so much of the wet stuff that Harry's foot wasn't able to grab a new hold. Callahan fell heavily on his back, his last round exploding toward the ceiling.

First he felt the shock of the hard metal slam his back, then he felt the beer soak into his jacket. His empty hand reached up and grabbed a crossbar on the catwalk bannister. He pulled himself up in time to catch the second deputy's gun butt in his neck.

The hard .357 revolver slammed deep into his skin, sending bolts of dark red and purple slashing across his vision. The blood was stopped cold in his neck for a second, creating the chill of shock and coming unconsciousness to Harry's brain. It reacted on automatic. Rather than pulling his other arm to cover his wound, a mental command brought his other arm around in a devastating roundhouse swing. His empty Magnum just happened to be at the end of that roundhouse swing.

The second deputy pulled his head back but it wasn't enough. The Magnum's barrel caught him just above the ear. There was a hard crack, then the second deputy spun over the catwalk's railing and fell eighteen feet to the brewery floor.

Harry leaned against the railing breathing hard and clawing in his pocket for an auto-load. He awkwardly pulled the device out just as the far door banged open and Sweetboy Williams stepped out.

Harry instantly told himself how to survive. He froze in place, making it quite clear his gun was empty. The hitman had to see the open chamber and hovering auto-loader. There was an endless second where the two men looked at each other and then Sweetboy motioned with his head. "Go ahead," he was saying. "I'll wait."

Before Harry could do anything, another door to Sweetboy's right flew open and Peter Nash fell out. He fell on his face, his cuffed wrists only partially breaking his fall. Right behind the ex-deputy was Sheriff Strughold. He took a second to squeeze a shot off at the dodging Sweetboy, then fell behind Nash's cringing form and tried to shoot anything that moved.

Harry jammed the six new rounds into his chamber and swung it shut while sliding behind another vat. The hitman simply ran back the way he had come. Sheriff Strughold hauled Nash up and, using him as a shield from Harry, went after the hitman.

Harry ran around the far side of the vat and raced to the door Nash had first fallen out of. It wouldn't do to burst through the door Sweetboy and the sheriff had disappeared into only to find both waiting, so he went in the other door.

It turned out to be all the same. Behind the first huge brewery room was another huge brewery room, only this time there was processing equipment under the cat-walks. This was where the beer was squirted into bottles, capped, and labeled. And this time there were no vats between the antagonists.

The open space caught them all by surprise. Nash twisted away from Strughold and hobbled toward Harry. Strughold pointed his gun toward Callahan. Sweetboy pointed his gun at Strughold.

The sheriff shot first just as the moment Nash weaved to the left. The bullet meant for Harry ripped into Nash's back, tore through a lung, and spun out through his chest. He fell at Harry's feet.

William's bullet went into Strughold's ear and immediately flew out the other one accompanied by a cloud of red spray. There didn't seem to be much else to get in its way. But when the sheriff fell, most of one side of his head fell first. The crooked lawman bent over the catwalk's railing like a dropped rag doll. His weight was enough to topple him over into the machinery below. His brains were bottled, capped, and labeled "Double Brewed, Double Delicious!"

Harry raised his weapon and shot at Sweetboy. The catwalk's railing got in the way again. The bullet screamed off it with a wicked howl. Sweetboy fired back. The bullet went over Harry's shoulder and blasted the glass out of the door behind him.

Before either could get off another shot, the cavalry arrived. A platoon of uniformed men burst into the room from the ground floor rear. It only took them a second to assimilate what was going on. Then it was every man for himself.

Harry jumped back through the door he had entered and kept running. Lying in wait for Sweetboy with a police army attacking was foolhardy at best, suicidal at worst. His only chance was to get out the way he had come. Harry leaped down the brewery stairwell one flight at a time.

As he reached the floor he heard Sweetboy crashing his way across the catwalk overhead. The hitman would only slow his pace to fire back the way he had come. Harry saw that the assassin now hefted two Magnums, one in each hand. Harry had to admit it was a good idea so he collected a fallen deputy's .357 just before the cop army attacked the room. Most of them went after Sweetboy on the catwalk, but some came in by way of the groundfloor doors. Harry slid out the side door before any of them spotted him.

With all deliberate speed, he made it back through the front entrance by way of the brewery museum. He was met by a crush of reporters, cameras, and high-ranking law officials. Harry dug through them, giving the thumb's-up signal to the police chief and Ted the Lieutenant as he went.

It was enough to get him by. He headed right for the sheriff's car. The keys were still in the ignition. Stupid sheriff. Harry got in, started it up, and took off. Since he had come in with Strughold, no one thought it strange he leave in Strughold's car.

Harry drove up Roosevelt Boulevard and onto Highway 81 like a madman. He was just wounded enough and just angry enough to play a hunch.

If he could get out of the brewery that easily, Sweetboy could probably get out some way as well. And Striker knew it. With both Callahan and Williams on the loose, the businessman would be smart to get out of town or dig himself in. Harry was counting on the fact that Striker didn't have time for the former.

The fact was that he had to get to Striker, Sweetboy or no Sweetboy. If he couldn't use the Mexican as a shield, his chances of getting the evidence out of Texas were back down to zero.

Nine

Harry just made it to the front of Striker's private road when both his front tires blew out. The sheriff's car careened crazily down the secluded path, sideswiping trees and running in the side ditches. Harry desperately attempted to control the speeding automobile.

He had just about got it to fly right when the windshield exploded. The police vehicle jumped the road completely, squealed across a rocky bunker on its front wheel rims, and smacked head-on into a tree.

Harry was on the floor, lying on the accelerator and brake. Since the car was already slowing when the glass flew in, he was only slightly dazed by the collision. He was more surprised by the friendly, smiling face at the open passenger's window. It was the face of Sweetboy Williams.

"Hi," the hitman said.

Harry glared at him until it became obvious that he was not a mirage, would not go away, and wasn't about to kill him. At least, not yet.

"Hi," said Harry back, dusting off some glass shards and gingerly crawling back to the front seat.

"Striker's inside," Sweetboy informed him. "He's turned the place into a fortress. All his available men have been called in for protection. It's going to take an army to get inside. Or you and me."

Harry sat up. He tried to open the door. It wouldn't budge. So he climbed out the window instead. He dropped to his feet across the crumbled car roof from Williams.

"I've got two .44s," the hitman continued affably. "You've got a .44 and a .357 on the seat there. What do you say, truce?"

Harry stared and scowled.

"I could have killed you rather than just stopping the car," Sweetboy explained. "And you need to get to Striker as much as I want to."

"I need him alive," Harry said.

"Alive or dead, it'll serve you either way. With Strughold dead, there'll be nobody to bring you up on charges."

"Their reports?"

"Locked in Striker's safe. All the rest of the police force knows that Strughold had been bragging about busting you. But so far he's produced nothing tangible."

"So I could just walk away," Harry reasoned.

"There's still Striker," Williams reminded him. "And me."

Harry considered his chances.

"Go ahead," Sweetboy said. "Try it. I'm willing."

Harry's hands kept away from his guns. "How are we going to get in?" he finally asked, waving a limp hand at the ruined police car.

"Come on," Sweetboy answered, walking up toward Striker's mansion.

Harry collected the extra .357 Python model on the front seat and followed the hitman up the winding, wooded road. He came around a corner to see Sweetboy sitting on the running board of a big beer truck.

"What took you so long?" the assassin asked sardonically. Suddenly it was very clear how Sweetboy had escaped from the brewery. It was the old "Purloined Letter" ploy. What would be the most natural vehicle leaving a brewery? Why, a beer truck, of course. Sweetboy had driven to Striker's house in a truck emblazoned with the motto: "A Brew As Big As Texas!"

Harry climbed up the passenger's side without comment. Sweetboy stood, then jumped back into the driver's seat. The inspector noticed a couple of bags crammed behind the front seat and a glove compartment bulging with ammunition.

"Help yourself," said the hitman, waving at the bullets as he put the truck into gear. "I've got some lighter loads for the .357."

Harry complied, keeping himself occupied by breaking open the second gun's cylinder chamber and digging through the shells for the right size. Although he tried not to, he couldn't help realizing that this was the biggest fight he had gotten involved with since World War II. He was preparing to either eradicate a large number of San Antonio's underworld or commit an extremely flamboyant suicide.

If Harry were somewhat reluctant, Sweetboy seemed raring to go. He was acting like the late sheriff had after arresting Harry. He was giving off a sense of holiday; a feeling that he was about to embark on the greatest fun of his life.

It was Sweetboy's wild West fantasy come true. Two men with six-guns about to take on a veritable army.

Well, that's what I get for leaving Frisco, Harry rationalized. Teamed up with a mad killer to attack a mansion. He wouldn't have been surprised if Sweetboy actually wanted to die in the coming firefight, but he himself had no intention of biting the dust. Harry slammed the .357's loaded cylinder back home with an angry conviction.

Sweetboy got the beer truck on and moving. They lurched up the private road, the hitman grinning like a gargoyle. "This is great," he said. "This is great."

Harry checked his surprise partner over. Sweetboy

was still in his all black outfit. The only difference between his appearance in the park was an extra holster attached to a gun belt around his waist. He had a shoulder holster like Harry's as well as a hunting knife in a scabbard on his left leg.

"I don't want to kill anybody," Harry told him. "I want Striker to give himself up."

"Fat chance," Sweetboy replied easily.

"I know," Harry admitted. "I'm just attempting to subtly tell you not to shoot unless shot at. Let's get out of this thing alive."

Sweetboy grinned his death-head grin again, taking a second to stare fullfaced at Callahan. "Fat chance," he said again.

Harry picked up on his meaning. Even if they blasted through Striker's house and came out the other side, they still had a matter to take up with each other. Neither was going to forget what the hitman had done to Boris Tucker and Candy McCarthy.

But for now it was just two big guys with four big guns banded together for survival.

"Hold it," said Sweetboy, motioning for Harry to take the wheel. Harry complied as the truck slowed down and the hitman stuck one of his Magnums out the driver's window. As they rolled slowly pass, Sweetboy shot the lens of a tree-mounted video camera apart.

"Well, now they know we're here," commented Harry.

"What do you think?" Sweetboy defended himself. "A truck from a brewery is going to fool anybody? Although you smell bad enough."

Harry sniffed. He smelled the beer that had soaked into his jacket. "OK, then," he shouted over the roar of the old engine. "Let's not keep them waiting."

Sweetboy pushed his foot to the floorboard. He ground the gears all the way up. The truck barreled down the road toward the main gate.

Harry took in as many details as he could as the vehicle grew ever nearer. The main gate was the usual ostentatious type: wrought metal twisted into a flowery shape laid across a thick steel frame. They looked like giant bathroom doors, only they locked in the middle and rose twelve feet from the road.

Beyond them was a large, perfectly manicured yard and then Striker's rambling Spanish-style mansion. On either side of the place and around the back were gardens rivaling those of Brackenridge Park.

Harry could see no more because the metal gate loomed in front of the windshield. Both men ducked down as the truck crashed through, hurling one side of the gate back and completely ripping the other side out of its stonewall mooring.

Sweetboy began to sit up again. "Stay down!" Harry warned just as a simultaneous barrage of gunfire blasted out from the house. It wasn't concentrated enough to do any major damage, but several small spiderwebs appeared in the windshield.

"OK," said Harry as both men warily sat up. Sweetboy started hauling the truck's wheel from side to side, making them into either a harder target to hit or a very drunk-looking truck. Harry watched the grounds carefully to spot any possible targets. Puffs of gunfire and pieces of lead continued to shoot out of five different ground-floor windows.

"Striker's office is in the back!" Sweetboy shouted as the truck tore across the lawn, throwing up big hunks of grass with its eight tires. "Let's see if I can drive all the way to it!"

The truck straightened and bore down on the manse's front door. Harry had to agree. It was a crazy thing to do, but he would have done it alone as well. Harry rammed his Magnum back into his holster and braced himself. Old "leadfoot" Williams gunned the engine again and drove right at the front stairs and front porch.

"Whooooo-weeeeeee!" Sweetboy screamed as the truck leaped up the steps, bowled across the stone porch and exploded through the front of the house.

Plaster, brick, adobe, and glass blasted in every direction. Furniture and furnishings spun everywhere. The truck kept on going. It careened off a marble column into the main hall. Sweetboy spun the steering wheel to avoid driving up the front steps. Instead the side of the wheels bounced off the bottom of the stairway and drove right through two more doors into the dining room.

The truck front pushed down the doors, taking a good section of the sculptured wood walls with it. Harry saw the truck hood accordion and what was left of the headlights ram into the engine. Then tables, cutlery, and china were flying everywhere. Harry saw one tabletop smash into a shotgun-wielding guard at the front window. Both of them went outside the hard way. The guard at the other front window scuttled into the unlit fireplace for protection.

Then the truck came out the other side of the dining room into the gigantic living room. It looked to be the size of a football field with a six-foot-high stone fireplace between two picture windows and two long couches lining one wall, a play area complete with pool table and a bowling alley against the other, and a sunken entertainment center in the middle.

The beer truck smashed through double French doors, slammed down three stairs that stretched all the way around the room, scraped against a circular stairway that led up to a balcony that also lined all four walls, then fell right into the entertainment area.

It was almost a perfect fit. Sweetboy slammed on the brakes and the vehicle slid across the floor and dropped down into the equipment-filled space. The front slammed against the front of the sunken area, stopping the forward movement. The rear of the truck dropped down to crush a giant video screen, a quadraphonic stereo system, a video recorder, and several smaller TVs.

The firefight didn't wait for the smoke to clear. Armed men behind the gaming tables, behind the couches and on the balcony started shooting. They had everything. As Harry threw open his door and dropped below the top of the sunken level, he saw AR-15 Sporters designed from the Colt M16, Ruger Mini-14, .223 carbines with twenty-round box magazines, thirteen-round, 9mm automatics, army forty-fives, and shotguns of all types.

But while the enemy had quantity, their shooting was hysterical. They just poured on the lead thinking that they'd hit something by sheer number alone. targets hadn't been Sweetboy and Dirty Harry, they ably would have been right.

Both men knew what to do. The more men firing the worse their chances were. Harry was on the couch and fireplace side while Williams was being pinned down by those among the adult toys. They ignored both, choosing to pick off the men on the balcony first. It afforded the men the least cover and the best angle to shoot from.

Harry kept the .357 in his left hand, his right jacket pocket filled with extra shells. His left pocket had all four of his auto-loaders, replenished from Sweetboy's glove compartment armory.

He fired with the aim only fear of God could create. The first Striker henchman fell back against a balcony bookcase, most of his stomach hanging out his back. A bullet plowed into the floor near Harry's face. He immediately swung his Magnum arm around to peg another balcony man, who fell over with a hole in the side of his neck.

Now it was time to get the guys on the ground level. A foolish fellow jumped up from behind the lefthand couch with a "Supermatic" auto-loading shotgun held at waist level. He tried to let Harry have three rounds, but Callahan was no longer where he was aiming. The pellets dotted the side of the truck as Harry rolled, came up six feet away, and shot the guy in the chest. The shotgun spun onto the couch and the guy flew out the window behind him.

Another shotgun owner popped up from behind the righthand couch. He also held the weapon at stomach level, so his shot ground into the floor two feet in front of Harry. The only damage that guy did was to sting Harry's shoulder with a couple of pellets that bounced. These guys never learn, Harry thought. You can't get any accuracy holding any rifle at waist level. But those hotshots see "Rifleman" repeats and they think they can do anything.

Harry brought the Magnum up to his eye level and blew the other man's head apart. He fell behind the couch. That finally reminded Harry why this firefight looked so familiar. It was like a penny-arcade rifle game played for keeps. Little targets pop up and you knock them down for points. Only this time if you lose you die.

In the few seconds he had before reinforcements arrived, Harry looked through the truck cab's window. Sweetboy was doing the same from the other side.

"All set?" Harry asked.

"Yeah. I think more's coming."

"Let's get out of here. I'll give them a diversion."

Sweetboy nodded, then both men scrambled out of the sunken area and raced for the closed doors on the other side of the room. Before they separated to take positions on either side of the two closed doors, Harry instructed through clenched teeth.

"On the count of four . . . both barrels into the gas tank."

"All right!" Sweetboy acknowledged.

The pair split up to take positions by each of the two doors leading out into the next room. Their timing was perfect. As soon as Harry rested his shoulder against the wall, the doors swung outward, effectively masking both him and Williams as another bunch of henchmen ran into the room.

None thought to look behind the doors. Instead they ran to their fallen comrades. Harry counted while aiming both guns at the smoking vehicle in the entertainment pit. What he was aiming at was the glove compartment. The gas tank was in the back and he couldn't hit it from that angle. He hoped Sweetboy had a better angle. He hoped he could detonate the ammo in the glove compartment, which, in turn, might find the gas tank. He hoped the whole room didn't wind up scattered all over San Antonio.

He reached four and fired. He didn't wait around to see what happened. He threw himself around the door and out the way the reinforcements had come in. He heard one shout behind him then his back was baked by a warm glow, the air pressure increased on his ear drums, a strange wind gripped his entire body at once, and he found himself flying.

Then he heard the explosion.

He was sliding across a brightly tiled hallway when he saw the flames lick out of the living room and pieces of the car and house started flying by. Harry crashed against the opposite wall, dropping his two guns in the process.

It didn't make any difference. No one would be doing much for the next few minutes. They were very lucky the room was as large as it was or they would have been killed as quickly as were the reinforcements.

As it was, the explosion's concussion blasted out every window in the room and took off most of the ceiling. Big holes appeared in the walls where hunks of the truck had traveled, and what was left of the walls were in flames. Bodies and parts of bodies littered both the front and back yards.

Harry felt hard pieces of something punching into the wall behind him. Without thinking he clawed his way to the nearest room which happened to be a sumptuous bathroom off the hall he had just flown down. He fell across the sink and onto the toilet as Sweetboy slammed up against the wall he had just left.

Harry watched the last remnants of the explosion course down upon the lying hitman through the open bathroom door. He heard the crackle of flames and the faraway wail of an automatic alarm. Although their detonating the truck was a dangerous maneuver, it was a fortuitous one. Not only had it wiped out most of the opposition in one fell swoop, it was sure to bring authorities. At least a while bunch of firemen.

Harry cautiously hazarded a glance out the bathroom door. The living room was completely filled with smoke. The hallway off it was littered with debris and blood. Sweetboy lay motionless under a pile of rubble. Harry wasn't so much interested in whether he was dead or alive as where his guns were. Harry found his own after ten seconds of concerted searching. Before he moved off, he tapped his inside jacket pocket. He heard the click of the plastic cassette within. He had lucked out. He hadn't lost the evidence. Now all he had to do was find Striker.

Harry shuffled past the hitman's still form and opened a battered door into a bedroom. Huddled together on the floor were four young women in maids' uniforms. By the bed in front of them were two more henchmen with guns.

It was a pretty classic confrontation. Both men grabbed for their weapons inside their jackets. Harry brought up both his pistols which were already in his hands and shot them. The one on the right was dead. The one on the left was badly wounded. Harry wasn't as used to the .357 model.

He walked over and kicked the wounded man's gun out of reach, then turned his attention to the quartet of pretty women. Each was Anglo, of various hair colors, and all were petrified with fear.

"Where's the boss?" Harry asked.

Misunderstanding him, the brunette, raven haired, and redhead pointed to the blond. "Aw, son-of-a-bitch!" she said.

"I'm not going to hurt you," Harry said, feeling more and more like he had stumbled into a John Wayne movie. "I just need to know where Striker is."

"He's in his office," said the brunette.

"Where is it?" asked Harry.

The women looked at each other, suddenly becoming all loyal and secretive.

"Come on, there isn't much time," Harry pressed.

"Through there," the blond said, pointing at a darker-colored, ornately sculptured section of the wall.

"How do I get in?"

"He has a little box that opens it," said the redhead. "He carries it with him."

"Great," Harry muttered.

"But I've seen him open it from the bed," the raven-haired girl piped up.

"I bet you have," cracked the blond.

"No, really," said the black-haired girl, hopping up

onto the canopied bed and reaching behind the headrest. "Here, look."

"Hold it," Harry demanded. "The rest of you get out of here," he instructed the women. They looked fearfully from the smoke pouring into the room from the living room back to Harry.

"But we don't have a way out," complained the blond.

Harry pointed the .357 over their heads and shot through a small, circular stained glass window on the front wall.

"Now you do," he said, cracking open the Magnum's cylinder. The shoot-out with the bedroom guards had used up his first six rounds. He shoved the .357 into his pant pocket and reloaded the Magnum. "Go on, get out." The girls started for the opening. "All except you," Harry pointed at the black-haired girl. She stood on her knees on the bed. She pointed to herself and mouthed the word "me?"

"Yeah," said Harry pulling out the Python revolver again. "When I nod, you open the door, then get out, all right?"

She mutely nodded. Harry waited until all but the blond had gingerly crawled out the front window before walking over to the darker wood panel on the wall. He crouched next to it, then nodded at the girl. She twisted her arm and the panel swung open.

Harry dived through, rolled, came up behind a white couch and pointed both guns over the top.

Hannibal Striker, also known as Edd Villaveda, was calmly sitting behind his desk, his hands in the prayer position in front of him.

"Inspector Callahan," he said casually.

Harry kept his position but relaxed his muscles somewhat. "You going to come along quietly," he said, well aware of the facetiousness, "or am I going to have to get rough?"

Striker laughed, his head bent toward the ceiling.

"They don't call you Dirty Harry for nothing, do they?" he inquired lightly.

Instead of answering, Harry stood up and put the Python back in his waistband. "You didn't call the cops before so they wouldn't interrupt your killing me. Would you mind calling them now?"

Striker didn't move. "We could still make a deal."

"I'm sick of your deals," Harry said, moving around the back of the couch. "They never pan out."

"All the charges dropped," Striker continued, his voice soothing. "The sheriff's reports of your resisting arrest and assaulting an officer are in my safe. I'll burn them. Here. Now. I'll even have Williams killed."

Harry moved slowly toward the desk. "You're under arrest," he told Striker.

"You could go back to San Francisco," the businessman went on, his voice a steady drone. "We could forget about all this. Things could go on as usual."

"No, we're going to the police station. You're going to be my shield until we find out who's on which side."

Harry was nearly at the desk now. Striker had been moving steadily back in his chair until his folded hands were on the very edge of the tabletop.

Then Sweetboy Williams slammed against the entrance wall, blood streaming down his face and both guns clenched in his hands.

"Watch it!" he barked.

Harry turned his head back just in time to see Striker grab for something under the desk. Harry dove forward just as the installed gun tore a line of bullet holes across the room.

Callahan landed across Striker's tabletop and slammed his body against the seated businessman. The shooting stopped long enough for the chair to fall back and both men slam to the floor.

Striker was up like a weasel, snarling and grabbing a 9mm automatic out of his desk. He shot at Sweetboy first, but the bullet only sent the hitman reeling back into the bedroom. The businessman's second bullet was a bit more precise. It hit Harry in the left thigh.

Callahan bellowed in pain as he arched his body on the floor to bring up the Magnum. The leg wound threw his own shot off. It smacked into the ceiling.

The businessman took the moment of confusion to charge toward the exit. Harry saw his feet flying forward from under the desk, then saw the white button on the right underside of the desk drawer. There was a red button across from it. Harry played a fast hunch.

Just as Striker neared the door, Harry slammed the barrel of his gun onto the white button. He had been right. The red button set off the booby trap. The white button closed the automatic door.

Striker, to his everlasting regret, had built the automatic door for speed. When he wanted it open or shut, he wanted it to open and shut *fast*. So now, when it slammed closed with Striker's right leg being in the bedroom and his left leg being in the office, it slammed closed on him.

The sliding door's slide punched Striker in the face as he turned toward the click of Harry's gun barrel against the button. He fell back, dazed, so the door was able to catch him against the few inches of the opening. He was stuck half-in one room and half-in the other.

If the truth be known, the door, with all its hydraulic power, was not enough to keep him there. With a little effort, Striker could have squeezed out one way or another. But he didn't have time.

Sweetboy Williams was aiming at him from one side and Dirty Harry Callahan was hobbling at him from the other. He screamed as they both fired at almost the same time.

Striker's head blew apart like a flower blossoming. The force of two .44 bullets burrowing into his skull at once all but decapitated him. Literal gouts of blood erupted from his neck like a scarlet fountain. Both men had to move back to avoid bathing in it.

Harry dropped heavily to the couch. His leg was throbbing from the high-powered bullet and his head was throbbing from everything. Through the pounding haze he heard sirens coming from far away. Either the police had finally decided to show up or someone had called the fire department. As he looked at the remnants of Striker's corpse he saw the plumes of smoke worming into the office from outside.

Then he heard something else. He heard Sweetboy William's laugh. The hitman couldn't get back into the office. He didn't know about the button behind the headboard. If he tried to get Striker's body out of the way, the door would quickly complete its closing. And if he hung around too long, he wouldn't be able to get away.

Harry started making a tourniquet out of his shirt while watching his blood stain the white couch and rug. The rug wouldn't mind. It was already decorated with most of Striker's insides.

"Hey," said a voice from the door.

Harry looked up. Sweetboy was smiling like a madman over Striker's headless form. He looked like one of those tourists who stuck their heads over a painted placard at a photographer's booth on the boardwalk. It was the hitman's head on the businessman's body.

"See you at John Wayne's graveyard," Sweetboy said. Then Striker's corpse was headless again.

Harry finished the tourniquet and hobbled behind Striker's desk. He looked out the bulletproof one-way window. He saw smoke rolling across the lawn, but no flames. The sirens must've been the fire department, he reasoned. They probably had the fire itself under control by now. And since he couldn't see any way to open the picture window, he sat in Striker's soft brown chair.

If I feel any heat before the firemen arrive, I'll think about how to get out, Harry figured. Until then, why bother?

Harry sat and silently looked out the window.

Ten

"It's over," said Captain Porter.

"Yeah," said Harry without much conviction.

They were sitting in Porter's office in the San Antonio Justice Building.

"The mayor himself reviewed your material and personally set up a task force excluding anyone found on the computer list. The material is being thoroughly processed and the courts have already promised us fast action. Warrants should be coming through very soon."

"Great," said Harry.

Porter was confused by the inspector's lack of enthusiasm. "You're off the hook," he told Harry. "You can go home."

"Uh-huh," said Harry, checking his leg for the third time since he'd sat down. The police surgeon had informed him that the 9mm bullet had thankfully passed through his thigh without hitting any major arteries or bones. He had been very lucky Striker had not been using hollow-points or everything from Harry's knee down would now be plastic.

Instead they had bandaged him up, gave him a cane to use temporarily, and let him go with Captain Porter. But ever since he left the hospital, he had been kneeding and twisting the leg, checking for himself just how bad it was.

"So," Porter said with a touch of perplexion, "what are you going to do now?"

Harry looked up from his leg. He remembered that he had heard that same question recently. Carol Nash's face swam up into his thoughts. Then her face was replaced by Peter Nash's dying one. And then his was replaced by Sweetboy Williams' head; grinning over Striker's lifeless body.

The hitman was waiting for him. Harry considered planning a trap with Captain Porter. But Sweetboy had escaped dozens of cops. He had escaped all his life. Only Harry's presence alone would make him stand and fight.

"What I meant was," said Porter, noticing Harry's faraway look, "when are you heading back to Frisco?"

Harry looked up at him. "Soon." He went back to his leg. "Soon."

"Fine . . . uh, fine," said the Captain, wondering how to get rid of the inspector. "Can . . . uh, one of my men drop you anywhere?"

"Yeah. Sure," said Harry, coming out of his funk somewhat. "I'll need my stuff at the Ramada Inn."

"Of course!" Porter said with relief, taking Harry's arm and leading him out of his office. "I'll get a car for you. Take care of yourself, Inspector, and be sure to say hello to your Captain Avery for me."

Harry went back to the hotel in silence. Only after Harry got back to his room did he fully recall that all his own stuff was in garbage cans at the airport. He found a men's store off the hotel lobby and bought an entirely new outfit. A tweedy brown jacket, a dull beige shirt, brown slacks, and shoes. It was his usual look.

He went back to his room. He slipped the three auto-loaders he had left into his left jacket pocket. He strapped on his .44 Magnum. He called the airport and arranged for passage back to California. He called the

166

Nash residence. No one answered. He checked a map. According to it, his immediate destination was a few miles down the road. He went back to the lobby and checked out.

He went outside and ignored the taxis. He wanted his wounded leg to be limber. He needed to know just how much it would handicap him. He started walking due west. Two and a half hours later he reached his destination. It was getting near dusk. The sky was a beautiful deep blue shot through with a rainbow of sunset colors.

And lying at the end of a grassy walk, sitting serenely amid bright spotlights, was the Alamo.

It was closed. No one was around. The five windows in front were barred over. The doors looked locked. Harry limped slowly over to the two wooden doors. He put the flat of his right hand against the left one. He pushed. It didn't budge. He moved his palm over to the right one. He pushed. It swung open.

Harry ignored the handsome stonework of the facade. He ignored the intricately detailed archway and the handsome grounds. He pulled out his Magnum and went inside.

The interior was about as impressive as the interior of the Taj Mahal. Somehow tourists always seem to think they're going to see something spectacular inside both. Well, Harry knew that the Alamo was just one of five different missions, built by Spanish Catholics in the 1700s. It consisted of a monastary and a church. It was named for the cottonwood trees around it. In Spanish, it translated as Alamo.

The battle of the Alamo had ended March 5, 1836, when the last of 182 men were killed by Antonio Lopez de Santa Anna's Mexican forces. A hundred and forty-five years later, it was just Harry Callahan and Sweetboy Williams.

The plain stone interior was illuminated by the spots outside. It cast squares of golden light in through the barred windows. Like all ancient things it smelled musty. Harry stood in the open doorway, his gun up.

"Come on in," he heard Sweetboy call.

167

Harry looked quickly around. He couldn't see him. So he did as the voice instructed. He closed the door behind him and pressed himself against the entry wall.

"How do you want to play this?" Sweetboy's voice asked.

"It's your call," Harry told him simply. He waited for what seemed like a long time. Sweetboy was taking his own sweet time deciding. He must've been deciding more than just how to handle the showdown. He must've been wondering whether he could trust Harry to go along with his wild West desires. The hitman knew Harry's nickname. He must've thought about that.

But whatever went through his mind during that time he did not share with Harry. Finally he came to a decision.

"We'll make it fair," Sweetboy's voice echoed through the dim, cavernous fort. "One auto-loader. One chance to draw, load, aim, and fire. All right?"

It was an absurd situation. Two men who hardly knew each other. Two men who had fought side by side. Two men who wanted more than anything else, to kill each other. Two men negotiating how they'd do it. If it wasn't so deadly, it would be laughable.

"All right," said Harry.

"Get ready," said Sweetboy. "I'm showing myself."

The hitman stepped out from the shadows of a tan-colored column. He was holding his Magnum the same way Harry was; barrel pointing at the ceiling, finger lightly on the trigger.

"All right," the hitman said, staying close to the column. "Open the cylinder." If Harry was going to cheat, now was the time to do it. With Sweetboy's Magnum open, he could quite possibly shoot him before the assassin could shut his chamber and fire back.

Harry moved his thumb, clicked open the cylinder, and swung it out. Sweetboy did the same. All twelve bullets slipped out of the upraised guns and clattered to the stone floor.

"Now," said Sweetboy, "lower the gun by your side." Both men brought their weapons down until they rested against their thighs.

"What about your cane?" Sweetboy asked.

Harry let it fall to the floor. It drifted down and clattered away.

"On the count of three," said Sweetboy. "Go for a speed-loader."

"One."

Harry felt sweat appear on his forehead. The San Antonio night was hot. The interior of the Alamo was hotter. His Magnum seemed to get heavier and heavier.

"Two."

His leg began to throb. He suddenly couldn't remember whether his jacket pocket had flaps or not.

"Three!"

Harry's right thumb was kicking the Magnum's cylinder open as his left arm dug into his jacket pocket. There was a flap in the way. His hand nearly ripped right through it. He felt an auto-loader in his fingers when a sudden, slashing pain lanced through his wounded leg.

That was it. He knew he'd never get the gun loaded in time. Without looking at Sweetboy's progress, he ran forward while pulling the speedloader out. A bullet grazed the back of his neck at the same moment he heard the hitman's gun boom. His running had saved him from an instant death. Now he had to fight a possible one in the near future. He heard Sweetboy coming after him. He forced his bad leg to keep moving.

He felt the shadow of a column cross his face. His leg was sending screams up to his brain. He pulled the auto-loader toward the open cylinder.

His leg collapsed under him, the auto-loader grazing against his thigh. The force was enough to dislodge all the ammo from its plastic prison. Another six bullets scattered across the floor.

Harry knew Sweetboy wouldn't be merciful this time. He had had his chance and blown it. He saw Sweetboy's shadow emerging from behind the column before the hitman himself appeared.

The assassin walked right into Harry's fist. Harry had pulled himself up, his arm already swinging as Sweetboy showed up. Williams stumbled back as Harry groped for the spilled bullets.

Sweetboy's vision cleared in time to see Harry ram a shell into his chamber. He brought his full Magnum up as Harry painfully propelled himself forward again. Sweetboy pulled the trigger as Harry hit his torso in a full body tackle.

The assassin's bullet went wild, and both men tumbled to the hard Alamo floor. Harry grabbed Sweetboy's gun wrist. Sweetboy grabbed Harry's. They rolled across the floor, teeth clenched with the effort.

Sweetboy applied all the muscle he could muster. His gun inched toward Harry's head. He saw Callahan's face covered with sweat, drops coursing across his face, over his lips, and off his chin.

Sweetboy's gun grew even closer to Harry's head. Through a supreme effort of will and muscle, Harry then stopped the hitman's arm cold. Sweetboy pulled the trigger anyway.

It was a rotten thing to do. The weapon boomed and the bullet blasted out practically in Harry's face. Men had been known to be blinded and deafened by getting too close to a firing gun.

Somehow, incredibly, Harry's eyes weren't lacerated by bullet shavings or gunpowder, and he maintained his grip on Sweetboy's wrist.

If anything, he bore down on the hitman's limb harder. And he started pulling his own gun toward the assassin's head.

Harry pulled the trigger. His own gun boomed. Sweetboy yelled in pain, his eyes closed. The hitman pulled his trigger again. Harry closed his eyes and averted his head.

Harry fired again. Tears were running out of Sweetboy's eyes and a single drop of blood fell out of his left ear. Sweetboy fired again.

Harry threw himself back from the report, found his footing, arched his back and dragged Sweetboy up with him. They stood shakily facing each other for a second, both guns pointed back at the ceiling.

Harry tore his wrist out of Sweetboy's grip and tried to bring his gun down. The hitman punched Harry's arm with a karate-like chop just as the inspector fired. The bullet singed Sweetboy's pant leg.

Sweetboy wrenched his own wrist from Harry's hand. Harry responded immediately by moving forward, sticking his leg between those of the hitman, throwing his hand forward, and shoving Sweetboy as hard as he could.

Williams tripped slightly, stumbled back, his arms flailing like windmills, and collided with another column. His eyes glazed as Harry brought up his gun again. He slid down the column just as Harry fired. The bullet smashed in the center of the column where Williams' head had been.

Sweetboy's eyes cleared, and he shot Harry in the left shoulder.

Callahan felt his feet leave the floor and a strange billowing sensation in his shoulder. He felt like he was floating upward in slow motion until his heels hit the floor and his head got too heavy. He fell all the way down to the concrete feeling absolutely nothing.

Then the pain started. He looked at his arm. He saw his left fist clenching and unclenching. It couldn't be too bad, he thought then. He saw his right hand cover the bloody shoulder wound. He felt the warm liquid on his palm. Then he realized he wasn't holding his gun.

He looked back. His Magnum lay ten feet away from him. He looked up. Sweetboy was pointing his Magnum at Harry's head. Sweetboy pulled the trigger.

The click reverberated through the dusty hall. Sweetboy's sixth bullet was in Harry's shoulder.

Harry tried to get up. By the time he made it, Sweetboy had run over and collected Harry's gun.

They faced each other a last time. Harry was slightly bent, his shoulder bleeding, his leg bleeding again and his breath coming in ragged, tortured gasps. Sweetboy was panting in both effort and anticipation. He stood straight, aiming the gun at Harry's head.

The hitman milked the moment. Harry just stared hard. A fleeting look of doubt crossed Sweetboy's face.

"I know what you're thinking," said Harry. Slowly. Quietly. "You're thinking, 'did he load five or six bullets?'

Well, to tell you the truth, in all the excitement, I kinda lost track myself.

"But being that this is a .44 Magnum, the most powerful handgun in the world, and could blow your head clean off, you have to ask yourself a question.

" 'Do I feel lucky?' "

Harry's stare hardened. His gaze narrowed.

"Well, do you?" he spat. "Punk."

Then he did an incredible thing. He straightened his back and crouched slightly. He positioned himself so that he was looking right down the Magnum's barrel. Then he closed the other eye.

Sweetboy was stunned. Harry was looking down the barrel so that if no bullet were in the chamber, he'd see it. He'd see daylight out the other end when he pulled the hammer back.

The hitman smiled and minutely shook his head. This cop was truly incredible.

He pulled the hammer back.

Harry smiled.

The smile froze Sweetboy in place. He saw, the hitman's brain screamed, he saw! Daylight, only five bullets. The whole confrontation turned over in the hitman's mind.

Harry ran forward, ignoring the pain and hit Sweetboy as hard as he could, driving his right fist into Williams' face, putting his whole torn body behind it.

Sweetboy flew backward almost as far as Harry had after getting shot. Only the assassin was able to hold onto the weapon. Harry, in the meantime, had run back to where Sweetboy had dropped his own gun.

The hitman awoke three seconds later to see Harry pulling his last speed-loader out of his jacket pocket. Sweetboy knew what he was planning to do. He was going to load the assassin's gun and kill the assassin with it. Sweetboy knew he didn't have enough time to reload Harry's empty gun.

In frustration, he pulled up the Magnum in his hand, pointed it in Harry's general vicinity and pulled the trigger.

He nearly died of shock when the revolver boomed

and bucked in his hand. The bullet flew past Harry's head—a full half-foot away from the target. Sweetboy saw Harry's smile again and realized what had happened.

The hitman had been bluffed. Harry hadn't seen daylight out the other end. He had seen the blackness of death ... the blackness of a bullet ready to blow him apart. And he had smiled at it as if it were empty.

Harry slammed the other Magnum's loaded cylinder shut with a savage satisfaction. He jerked his head at the useless weapon in Sweetboy's hands.

"*Now* it's empty," Harry informed him, then shot him in the face.

No, they didn't call him Dirty Harry for nothing.

MEN OF ACTION BOOKS

DIRTY HARRY
By Dane Hartman

He's "Dirty Harry" Callahan—tough, un-orthodox, no-nonsense plainclothesman extraordinaire of the San Francisco Police Department... Inspector #71 assigned to the bruising, thankless homicide detail ... A consummate crimebuster nothing can stop—not even the law! Explosive mysteries involving racketeers, mur-derers, extortioners, pushers, and sky-jackers; savage, bizarre murders, accom-plished with such cunning and expertise that the frustrated S.F.P.D. finds itself without a single clue; hair-raising action and violence as Dirty Harry arrives on the scene, armed with nothing but a Smith & Wesson .44 and a bag of dirty tricks; un-bearable suspense and hairy chase se-quences as Dirty Harry sleuths to unmask the villain and solve the mystery. Dirty Harry—when the chips are down, he's the most low-down cop on the case.

MEN OF ACTION BOOKS

THE HOOK
By Brad Latham

"The Hook" is William Lockwood, ace insurance investigator for Transatlantic Underwriters—a man whose name derives from his World War I boxing exploits, whose hallmark is class, whose middle name is violence, and whose signature is sex. In the late 1930s, when law enforcement was rough-and-tumble, The Hook is the perfect take-charge man for any job. He combines legal and military training with a network of contacts across America who honor his boxing legend. He's a debonair man-about-town, a bachelor with an awesome talent for women—and a deadly weapon in one-on-one confrontations. Crossing America and Europe in pursuit of perpetrators of insurance fraud, The Hook finds himself in the middle of organized crime, police corruption, and terrorism. The Hook—gentleman detective with a talent for violence and a taste for sex.

COMING SOON FROM
MEN OF ACTION BOOKS

BEN SLAYTON: T-MAN
by Buck Sanders
Ben Slayton is one of only two men in the U.S. government privy to the most sensitive classified intelligence of all law enforcement agencies from the C.I.A. to Interpol. He operates in absolute secrecy and can change identities like a chameleon. A much decorated Vietnam veteran, he has a talent for weaponry and commando tactics. Based on actual experiences of T-men, Slayton travels over the world in a deadly chessgame with anarchists, political zealots, outlaw barbarians, and would-be presidential assassins.

S-COM
by Steve White
They are the elitest private army in a tinderbox world where the ultimate secret weapon is the highly-paid mercenary. To Third World nations embroiled in revolution, to international corporations bent on global exploitation, to superpowers with imperialistic designs, they are the most sought-after and most effective fighting force to secure. They have no allegiances; their services go to the highest bidder. And the four men and one woman of S-Com have a perfect record in the business of international espionage, terrorism, and guerilla warfare.

To order, use the coupon below. If you prefer to use your own stationery, please include complete title as well as book number and price. Allow 4 weeks for delivery.

WARNER BOOKS
P.O. Box 690
New York, N.Y. 10019

Please send me the books I have checked. I enclose a check or money order (not cash), plus 50¢ per order and 20¢ per copy to cover postage and handling.*

_____ Please send me your free mail order catalog. (If ordering only the catalog, include a large self-addressed, stamped envelope.)

Name_____

Address_____

City_____

State_____ Zip_____

*N.Y. State and California residents add applicable sales tax.